OTHER BOOKS BY *Donna Jo Napoli*

CHANGING TUNES

Donna Jo Napoli

CHANGING
TUNES

DUTTON CHILDREN'S BOOKS ▮ NEW YORK

I THANK *Lucia Monfried, Emily Rando, Richard Tchen, and my family, especially Barry, Nick, and Robert, for help on various drafts of this story. And I thank Ken Williams and Nick Furrow for discussing their feelings about music with me.*

Library of Congress Cataloging-in-Publication Data
Napoli, Donna Jo, date.
Changing tunes / by Donna Jo Napoli.—1st ed.
p.   cm.
Summary: Ten-year-old Eileen's life changes drastically when her father separates from her mother and moves out, taking with him the piano on which she is used to practicing every day.
ISBN 0-525-45861-1 (hc)
[1. Divorce—Fiction.   2. Musicians—Fiction.]   I. Title.
PZ7.N15Ch   1998   [Fic]—dc21   98-10034   CIP   AC

Published in the United States by Dutton Children's Books,
a member of Penguin Putnam Inc.
375 Hudson Street, New York, New York 10014
Designed by Amy Berniker
Printed in USA   First Edition
10 9 8 7 6 5 4 3 2 1

For
Eric and Nate Ross, Zach Tollen,
and Cam Winton

Contents

███

CHANGING
TUNES

one
THE PIANO

*E*ileen twisted her hair around her finger. She thought about home. About what would and wouldn't be there when she opened the back door. About her father.

Stephanie pinched her.

"Ouch!" Eileen inspected the red pinch mark on her arm. "That hurt."

"Well, at least I have your attention now." Stephanie scratched her elbow through the big hole in her yellow sweater and did a little skip. Her loose shoelaces flopped on the sidewalk. "Yes, it's better not to have everything you want. And don't you think Milo's new backpack is gross, with all those zipper pockets and those fat padded straps?" Stephanie walked ahead quickly. "Yes, it's better the way things are. Both things."

Eileen shifted the matted straps of her old backpack and hurried to catch up. "Both what things?"

"Milo's backpack and Mandy's party, of course. She's going to have boys this year and dancing, and she didn't invite us." Stephanie spoke matter-of-factly. "That's actually better, much better not to have everything, you know."

Eileen didn't know. "I think having everything you want is pretty good."

"That's only because you don't have everything you want. If we went to every party that came along, we'd get apathetic. Nothing would be fun. Here." Stephanie pulled a mashed sandwich out of her lunch bag. "Want half?"

Eileen wondered what *apathetic* meant. She took the sandwich, expecting salami with lettuce and mustard. Or maybe roast beef with mayonnaise. Or tuna salad. Stephanie could have her pick of whatever sandwich anyone brought, because everyone was always ready to trade with her. Eileen took a bite. "Hey. It's jelly."

"I know. I didn't trade today. I wanted it just for us— for us to share."

Eileen smiled. "Thanks. I wish my mother would let me bring jelly sandwiches. Then I could trade, too."

"Well, I'm glad other mothers don't let their kids bring jelly. Otherwise I'd have to go through a lot of trouble making a decent lunch every day." They reached the corner where their ways parted. Stephanie stopped and tied her shoelaces.

"Is your mother still nagging you about your laces?" asked Eileen.

"Yeah." Stephanie stood up and brushed off her hands. "Sometimes I wish I had a mother like yours."

"Like mine?"

"She lets you do anything you want," said Stephanie.

"She wouldn't like it if I went around with my laces untied."

"How do you know?"

Eileen thought of that morning and how she had watched her mother tuck her white blouse into her blue pleated skirt and then smooth it all with both hands. Mom had looked like a magazine model. Mom always looked perfect. "I just know. Anyway, she'd never let me bring jelly sandwiches."

Stephanie nodded and looked away for a moment, up the long row of front yards toward Eileen's house. "Can I come over?"

Eileen shook her head. "Not today." Today Eileen

wanted to face what she would find at home herself. But she wouldn't tell Stephanie that. "I'm working on a new piano piece."

"That stinks, having to practice all the time. I never practice."

"Oh, but I love it," said Eileen.

Stephanie wiggled her nose. "I guess if I was really good at something, well, I guess I might love practicing, too."

"I'm not all that good," said Eileen.

"You won the state award last year."

"County." In her head Eileen could hear the piece she had played: Mozart's "Polonaise." "And I didn't win. I only got second place."

"Whatever." Stephanie shrugged. "I should get home, anyway."

Eileen fiddled with her jacket buttons. She was grateful Stephanie didn't ask why she couldn't practice piano after dinner like she usually did, instead of now. At the same time, she almost wished Stephanie had asked that.

"It's been a long time since I've come over to your house," said Stephanie.

Eileen bit her bottom lip. She knew exactly how

long it had been: two weeks. Ever since her parents had told her.

Stephanie pulled her sweater tight around her. "Bye now." She ran off.

Eileen wanted to run with her. She wanted to ask Stephanie if she could put a sleeping bag on her bedroom floor and just stay there for a while. Like ten years. She wanted to sit in Stephanie's kitchen and listen to Stephanie chatter on and just feel safe in the blanket of words.

Stephanie reached the next corner and crossed the street. She turned and waved at Eileen.

The back door was locked. Eileen tried it again. Locked, on this of all days. She ran around to the front and rang the bell.

She slipped her heavy backpack off and laid it on the welcome mat. Why was Mom taking so long? Eileen wanted to get inside and look around. She rubbed her shoulders where the straps of the backpack had dug in. Come on, Mom, she thought.

Eileen rang the bell again.

The mailbox was full. Eileen looked through the envelopes. Of course she wasn't expecting a late invitation to Mandy's party. But sometimes Grandpa sent her notes. But Grandpa's big scrawl wasn't there. Eileen shut the mailbox. Where was Mom?

Eileen rang the bell and hammered at the door with her fist. "Mom!" She kicked the door.

"Ah, there you are," called Mrs. Tilly, running over from next door.

Eileen watched Mrs. Tilly rush along in her black-and-white flowered dress and felt a hot flush of embarrassment go up her neck and into her cheeks; Mrs. Tilly had seen her kicking the door, acting like a little kid. She forced a smile.

Mrs. Tilly smiled back. "Your mom had to go out and she asked me to watch for you. I've got the key. I'll let you in."

"Thank you," Eileen mumbled. She picked up her backpack and stepped aside.

Mrs. Tilly opened the door. "Do you want me to stay with you till your mom gets home?"

"Oh, no. I'm fine alone." Eileen stood up tall and held out her hand. "I'll put the key inside."

"Of course. You're in fifth grade now, aren't you?" Mrs. Tilly handed Eileen the key. "Time does fly." She adjusted her glasses. "Would you like to come over for a snack?"

All Eileen wanted to do was get inside and shut the door and see—see for herself what the house was like now. "I've got tons of homework. Thanks anyway." She stepped inside.

"Well, I'm right next door if you need anything." Mrs. Tilly walked back across the grass. Her dress seemed to flow around her. Eileen shut the door and turned around.

The living room looked the same, only even neater than usual, if that was possible. Eileen walked past the coffee table, covered with organized stacks of magazines, through to the kitchen. She slung her backpack onto the kitchen table and put the key on the counter beside it. She slipped off her jacket and let it drop on the floor.

Then she went upstairs to what was now Mom's room. She opened the closet, warning herself that it would be half empty. It wasn't. Daddy's things were gone, but Mom's things were spread out, filling the closet, with space between each hanger.

Eileen went back downstairs and slumped onto the couch. From this position she could see that the bookcase under the window was almost empty. Well, who cared? Those books never interested Eileen, anyway. They were about politics and stuff. And now she noticed that the mantelpiece was clear. Daddy's wood carvings from his travels after college were gone. All of them. The mantel-piece was bare.

Eileen reached out her foot and knocked the magazines off the coffee table. That was more like it. A house should be messy. Otherwise it would look like no one lived in it. And people lived in this house, even if Daddy had moved out. Eileen stood up and kicked a magazine across the rug.

She thought of her homework. Science and math. Then she thought of the wood carvings that used to be on the mantelpiece. She never really liked any of them. In fact, Eileen didn't care one bit that Daddy had taken his things. Not one bit. So this restless feeling didn't make sense. But as long as she felt like this, she knew she wouldn't be able to concentrate on her homework.

So she decided to practice the piano first. After all, that's what she'd told Stephanie she was going to do. That would get her feeling right again. She'd play quick and clean today—she could feel it in her fingers already. She went into the piano room.

The piano was gone.

Eileen stood in the doorway, stunned. Through the thin veil of unshed tears she looked at the bare spot where the piano used to stand. A spasm went through her shoulders. Her ears felt cold. She was aware of the blunt silence of the room.

She blinked. Funny thing was, he'd said on the phone last night that the reason he was telling her that he'd be taking his things was so that she'd expect it. He didn't want unexpected things to happen to her. He wanted her to be prepared. That's what he said.

But he hadn't mentioned the piano.

His taking the piano meant it was part of his stuff. Eileen had never thought of the piano as his stuff. It was the piano. The family piano. She'd played on it since she was five. It was as much hers as it was his. Okay, sure, he'd been playing on it longer, since before she was born, but just because he was older was no reason why the piano should be his.

The piano was his.

What else? What else had she thought was family's that was really just Daddy's?

Eileen's ears burned now, and her eyes burned. She blinked faster. It wasn't that bad. She had lived through worse. After all, Daddy had stopped coming home two weeks ago. He had an apartment now. What difference did it make that today was the day he finally moved his stuff out? She'd known Daddy's stuff would be gone when she got home. She'd thought about it all day. He had prepared her. So the piano was gone. Who cared? It needed to be tuned, anyway. And now she wouldn't have to practice Eckstein's boring exercises. She could think of that. No more Eckstein. She could think of that and her eyes would stop burning.

No more Eckstein.

And no more Mozart. Or Chopin. Or Schubert. Or Mendelssohn. No more Scott Joplin. No more wonderful composers.

And no more playing after dinner with Daddy listening. But, then, Daddy hadn't been there to listen for the past two weeks anyway. So it didn't matter. Nothing mattered.

Eileen dropped on her knees to the floor. Her fingers traced the geometric design of the rug.

"I'm sorry," came the whisper.

Eileen jumped up and whirled around.

Mom put her arms tight around her. "I'm sorry, baby."

Eileen pulled away from her mother and stood shaking. She squeezed her eyes shut so she couldn't cry. When she opened her eyes again, she said, "I guess I won't be taking piano lessons anymore."

"Of course you will." Mom raised both eyebrows and looked at Eileen firmly. "You most certainly will, Eileen."

"I can't practice without a piano."

"Lots of children take piano lessons without owning a piano. All you need is a piano you can use."

"I don't want to go to my friends' houses to use their pianos," said Eileen fiercely.

"You don't have to." Mom sat down calmly in the red chair by the bookcase. She hadn't even put her purse down yet. She clutched it now. "I talked to your school principal. I've arranged for you to use the piano in the school auditorium after school every day." She crossed her legs and swung her top foot tensely.

Eileen looked at her mother's flat-heeled brown shoes and hated them. She hated everything sensible and reasonable. When she was old enough, she'd wear four-inch high heels. Maybe five-inch. "What about weekends?"

"You spent last weekend at your father's. And you know we've agreed that you'll spend every other weekend there. You can practice at his place. Then on the weekends that you're here, you can take a rest from practicing. We'll need those weekends for you and me to spend fun time together, anyway."

Eileen clenched her teeth. "You have all the answers."

"That's not true, Eileen. I don't have any answers. I'm just trying."

Eileen looked at her mother and felt the tears wanting to burst out again. She wouldn't let them. She'd never let them. She'd never give in. She shook her long brown hair and looked at the ceiling. At the bookcase. At the window. And then at her mother again. Her mother, with every strand of hair in place, every part of her perfect.

"You give it a try too, Eileen." Mom's face was immovable, like a mask. But her voice cracked. "Please."

Eileen stiffened with anger. A try. Adults always change things. Do whatever they want, whenever they want. And kids are supposed to try.

two

I

BEETHOVEN

The next day Eileen sat in social studies class and looked lazily around the room. This was the end of the day, and it was project time: everyone had chosen a country, and they were supposed to find something about that country that they had some special attachment to. Eileen peered over Milo's shoulder. In shaky blue letters across the construction-paper cover of his project he had printed WEAPONS OF URUGUAY. Balanced at the edge of his desk was a volume of the classroom encyclopedia opened to *Weapons*, and Milo had made a list: *bolas, spear, bow and arrows, mace*. Mace? Milo was as short and skinny as Stephanie. Eileen pictured him grabbing a huge metal club with spikes on the end of it and reeling backward under the weight. She giggled.

"What's so funny?" whispered Stephanie from across the aisle.

Eileen pointed. Stephanie craned her neck and smiled.

Eileen looked down at the white paper on her own desk and concentrated on getting Mozart's curls right. She had drawn him sitting at a piano, leaning forward as he played. Eileen's project was about Germany and composers. Eileen drew in the third pedal on the piano. Then she looked across at Milo again. He was putting the finishing touches on a drawing of a sword. It was good.

The bell rang. "Okay, put your projects away, please. Clean up quick and go play." Mr. Kressler smiled. "Thanks for the good day, kids."

Eileen liked that about him. She'd never had a teacher before who thanked the class at the end of the day. But Mr. Kressler always did. Her mother said probably it was because he was a Quaker.

Eileen followed Milo to the shelves at the side of the class, where everyone had a spot reserved just for projects. She put hers carefully in place. "Your weapons look good, Milo."

Milo looked at Eileen in surprise. "Huh?"

"I like your project."

"Oh." Milo looked at Eileen's drawing on the shelf. "Your piano looks real." He screwed up his face. "But the woman looks sort of like a man."

Eileen laughed. "It is a man. He's got a wig on. They wore wigs when he lived. That's Mozart. He wrote operas and symphonies and stuff."

"So why'd you draw him at a piano?"

"He wrote good piano music too."

"Oh, yeah, you play piano. I remember from last year, in the spring concert." Milo grabbed his backpack and left without putting it on his back.

Eileen took her jacket off her hook at the back of the classroom and slowly put it on.

"Guess what my project's on," said Stephanie.

"Small boats," said Eileen.

"You saw," said Stephanie.

Eileen nodded. "What country?"

"Small boats and Italy. I just finished reading *The Silent Gondolier*. You have to read it. They still use gondolas in Italy, but *sandalos* have just about disappeared."

"What's a *sandalo*?" asked Eileen.

"It's a sort of short gondola. Come over to my house and I'll show you a wood model of one. My father borrowed it from a man at work just so I could see it. It's delicate, but you're careful, so I'll let you hold it."

"Not today," said Eileen, pulling at the edges of her jacket.

"Why not?" Stephanie examined her hands and bit at a hangnail. "You haven't come over for days . . . weeks." She looked up at Eileen. "Want me to come over to your house instead?"

"I'm not going home." Eileen lowered her eyes to her jacket buttons. "You go ahead."

"Why not? Where are you going?"

"No place interesting." Eileen pulled her backpack over one shoulder. There was no point putting it on properly when she would have to take it off again in a few minutes. She looked at Stephanie's concerned face. Maybe now was the right time to tell Stephanie. Yes, Eileen could do it now. She could. Her heart beat fast and her jaw felt heavy and thick. She took a deep breath. "Stephanie—"

"You shouldn't hang your backpack over one shoulder. Bonni—you know, the school nurse—she said that causes scoliosis. That girl Laurel, in the other fifth-grade class, got it. Adolescence is hard enough without being a pariah because you're all funny-looking." Stephanie put her hand over her mouth for a moment and seemed lost in thought. Then she reached out and held the loose strap of Eileen's backpack for her.

Eileen obediently pushed her arm through, wondering why Stephanie liked using big words so much.

"You have great hair, you know," said Stephanie.

Eileen hadn't thought much about looks lately. She examined Stephanie now. "You have good skin and special eyes."

Stephanie ran both hands over her cheeks from the nose outward and looked serene. She untwisted the strap of Eileen's backpack with a satisfied smile. "So where are you going?"

"The auditorium," said Eileen. She met Stephanie's eyes. "I'm going to practice the piano."

"But why?"

Why? Stephanie obviously was thinking about twisted backs and great hair and eyes. Eileen's news didn't fit now. "I'll tell you later. I'm in kind of a rush now."

"You've got a secret, don't you?"

Eileen turned and walked toward the auditorium.

"I bet you're going to play something special in the Halloween Day pageant, aren't you?" called Stephanie after Eileen's retreating back. She laughed. "I knew they'd pick you. You're the best piano player around. Well, I'll go catch up with Suzanne. She bought some Krazy Glue, and we thought we might make little dolls out of stones, gluing them together, you know. And little stone houses for them. And chairs and tables and dogs and fishbowls. A little stone world. Maybe you can come do it with us to-morrow."

Eileen refused to look back at Stephanie. A little stone fishbowl? She wondered if Stephanie would keep talking until Eileen was out of sight. But suddenly Stephanie's words stopped, and Eileen could hear her footsteps going down the hall in the other direction, loose laces slapping the linoleum.

Eileen ran ahead and turned the corner. She stopped in front of the closed auditorium door.

Yes, Eileen had a secret, but nothing so nice as what Stephanie had guessed.

In first grade, Stephanie was the first person Eileen ever had over to spend the night. They went to bed when Mom said—at eight o'clock. They were stupid then; now they always stayed up till midnight on a sleep-over.

In second grade, they started piano lessons together, and even now they walked to Mr. Gilbert's house after school every Tuesday for their lessons. Stephanie went first while Eileen waited. Then Stephanie would wait for Eileen. Eileen's father had taught her for two years before that, so she was way ahead of Stephanie on the piano. But that never mattered to them.

In third and fourth grades, they were in different classrooms, but that hadn't mattered either. They met at recess every day and swapped desserts at lunch, unless, of course, one of them had packed a special treat. Stephanie loved Oreos, and whenever she brought them, Eileen would never ask to swap. Eileen loved Fig Newtons. Stephanie never asked to swap those.

Now in fifth grade they were back in the same class, together again all day long.

They fought now and then. Eileen was jealous when Stephanie got her puppy in fourth grade. And it was awful when one of them was invited to a party and the other wasn't, but that hardly ever happened. And, anyway, you had to expect problems. You had to learn how to argue and make up. Otherwise you'd just leave each other. Be a quitter.

Like people who get a divorce.

Eileen lifted her chin in defiance. She wasn't a quitter. She wouldn't quit on Stephanie. Not after all they'd been through. They told everyone they were best friends.

Eileen looked up and down the deserted hall. She put her hand on the long metal bar that opened the thick auditorium door, but she didn't press. She leaned her forehead against the door and wondered if Stephanie would still say she was her best friend if she knew Eileen's father wasn't living at home anymore. Oh, it wouldn't matter to Stephanie what Eileen's parents did. That was the stupid part of this whole thing—Stephanie wouldn't care at all. No, the problem was the deception. If Eileen had told Stephanie two weeks ago, when Daddy first left, she was sure Stephanie would have hugged her and tried to cheer her up. But Eileen hadn't told anyone.

She had meant to. It was the first thing she did, picking up the phone in the kitchen, wishing with all her might that she had a phone in her bedroom so no one could listen in, dialing the number she could have dialed in her sleep. But then her mother came downstairs and went into the living room, and Eileen hung up just as Stephanie's voice said, "Hello?"

The next day Eileen had planned to tell Stephanie after school, on the way home. But Stephanie talked about happy things. Eileen's news would have ruined the mood.

By the third day, Eileen's mouth went cotton dry at the very thought of talking about it. She needed to tell

Stephanie. She wanted Stephanie's comforting words. But she didn't tell her. And with each passing day, it became more and more difficult to imagine telling her.

And now two weeks had passed.

Eileen lifted her head away from the door and looked up and down the deserted hall. She realized she must have been standing there a long time, because everyone was gone. She pressed down on the metal bar. The door swung open easily.

The lights were out, and the auditorium seemed bigger in the dark. Scary, almost. It smelled strange—dry and empty. Eileen felt like she didn't belong there. She couldn't remember ever going in the auditorium without her whole class.

The piano was in front of the stage and off to the right. Eileen took her piano books out of her backpack as she walked down the aisle. She placed them carefully on the old upright, opening the Eckstein first. She sat on the bench without taking her jacket off. The bench was too far out. She lifted her bottom a little and tried to pull it in under her. It wouldn't budge. Eileen got up, stood behind the bench, and pushed it into place. It was heavy—a lot heavier than hers. Than Daddy's. She sat down again.

It took her eyes a few minutes to adjust to the dim

light. In the meantime, she played Burgmüller's "Le Courant Limpide" by heart. The keyboard action surprised her. She barely had to press down at all, it was so loose. It felt like the whole piano was held together by a frayed rope, and if she pressed her fingers too hard, it would all come apart. Rickety, old, awful thing.

If the piano was going to sound this bad, it was better no one was there to listen to her practice.

She finished and put her hands in her lap while she examined the keyboard. The keys were yellowing and a few were chipped. She rubbed the chipped edges. They were dull, as though they'd been smoothed by thousands of fingers over the years. They were disgusting and dirty. She could barely stand to touch the keys, now that she'd looked at them closely. But she had no choice. Eileen put her hands back in place and played the song again. This song was supposed to sound light and flowing, like clear water. It didn't. It kind of bounced, jerkylike. Eileen doubted she could ever master the action of these keys enough to get a rippling sound out of the old piano.

Next, she played Burgmüller's "La Chasse" with all its crescendos. That was fun in spite of the ancient piano. And, finally, Mozart's "Polonaise," the piece she'd played when she won second prize. It started soft and went to loud and pulled her swirling through the repeat, then on to loud and soft and loud and another repeat, then a quick, loud finish. Eileen could make that piece terrific no matter what piano she played on. She lifted her hands with a flourish. The auditorium rang with the final notes.

All right, time to buckle down to the things Mr. Gilbert had assigned for that week. She fingered the music book Daddy had given her for her birthday. Daddy played mainly dramatic songs, things by Beethoven. But now and then he'd burst into something light and jazzy—something like Scott Joplin, which sounded so easy but was really so hard. Before Daddy had moved out, he and Eileen had played little snatches of Joplin songs together—not the original versions, because they required a long reach—just arrangements for smaller hands, but good arrangements. Eileen took the right hand and Daddy took the left hand. And then Eileen had convinced Mr. Gilbert to start her on "Maple Leaf Rag." Daddy didn't know about it. Eileen had planned to surprise him one day soon. Maybe at Thanksgiving.

She stared at the book now. Then she put it aside. She would save "Maple Leaf Rag" for last and do the boring stuff first.

Eileen pounded out her scales three times each, then

played Eckstein's study No. 14 slow, then fast, then staccato. Her wrists didn't even ache. If she worked on this horrible dirty old piano too much, she'd lose her strength. She wouldn't be able to play on Daddy's piano anymore.

Her eyes could see in the auditorium easily now. The stage was empty. Against the left wall stood Mr. Poole's broom. He was the school custodian. Over on the floor pushed against the wall near the exit doors was the big lost-and-found box. A jean jacket dangled over the edge, more out than in. About three-fourths of the way down the center aisle there was a crumpled piece of paper. Besides that, the auditorium was empty—just Eileen, the old piano, and rows and rows of seats.

Eileen turned her eyes back to the music books and opened to "Für Elise," a Beethoven piece that her father loved. He had taught it to her last spring, but she hadn't played it for a while. This morning she had put it in her backpack along with the other piano books, feeling good about it—feeling like she'd enjoy remembering playing this for Daddy. But here, in the semi-dark of this auditorium, on this nasty old piano, she didn't feel so good about it anymore. Who was this Elise woman anyway? What was so unusual about her that someone would want to write a song just for her? And what did Daddy like about this song? Eileen didn't think it was so special. In fact, she now realized she didn't even like it.

Eileen slammed the cover over the keys. The bang was so loud it made her jump. She put all her other music books into her backpack and grabbed the Beethoven book. She tried to rip the book in half, but it wouldn't tear.

There was a tall trash can near the side exit door. Eileen ran to it and shoved the Beethoven book through the lid. The lid swung crazily, creaking loudly as Eileen ran out the exit.

Eileen could hear the creaking in her head halfway home. She put her hands over her ears and kicked the dry oak leaves.

three

THE TIGER

The next morning Eileen hid behind the hedge and peeked out at the sidewalk.

"Eileen, dear. What are you doing?"

Eileen jumped around. "Oh, Mrs. Tilly, hello. I'm going to surprise my friend Stephanie. Don't give me away."

Mrs. Tilly hunched over and rubbed her hands together like a conspirator. "Of course," she whispered. "I just wanted to ask you to stop by after school today."

"Okay," Eileen whispered back.

"Bye now," whispered Mrs. Tilly, waving.

Eileen watched Mrs. Tilly hurry back into her house

before she remembered that after school today she was supposed to go to the auditorium to practice piano again. Well, all right, she'd be a half hour late to Mrs. Tilly's. That was okay. Mrs. Tilly probably didn't keep track of time anyway.

Eileen turned back to watching the sidewalk. Stephanie was in sight now.

"Boo!"

Stephanie jumped back. Then she saw Eileen and laughed. "What are you going to be for Halloween?"

"I don't know. Maybe a ghost," said Eileen. "What about you?"

"I'm going to be a tiger. You should see my costume. My mother said that since this will be my last Halloween as a kid, you know, 'cause in middle school people don't trick-or-treat and stuff like that, since it's the last time, it should be special. She's been working on it for a week. The fur is luxurious and looks good, even though it's fake. But fake fur is better than real because it doesn't smell when it gets wet." Stephanie skipped a few steps. "Weren't you a ghost last year?"

"Yeah," said Eileen, wondering how real fur smelled when it got wet.

"So don't you want to be something different? Suzanne's going to be a devil for Halloween. So don't you want to be something else?"

"Huh? I'm not going to be a devil."

"I know," Stephanie said in an exasperated voice. "I mean don't you want to be something besides a ghost again?"

"I don't know." Eileen tried to keep her voice light and happy. "My mom's pretty busy these days. I don't think I'll ask her about a new costume."

"What's she busy with?"

"She's looking for a new job." Eileen pulled dry leaves off a bush hanging over the sidewalk. "Her old one is part-time."

Stephanie nodded wisely. "Looking for more money?"

"Yeah."

"We've been through that. When my dad changed jobs last year, that was so he could get more money. Now he stays at work late every night, but he got a raise, so he's happy. It didn't do me any good, though." Stephanie shook her head in disgust. "He still won't get me a new bedroom set."

"You want a whole new set? I thought all you wanted was one of those fancy beds with a top."

"A canopy bed. And there's a table with a little bench that goes with it. And a bureau with gold painted trim.

The whole thing is fabulous." As Stephanie talked, she moved her hands to show the shapes. "That's what I want. We could have the best sleep-overs."

"It must cost a lot."

"Sure it does," said Stephanie. "My dad said he'd pay me if I worked every night for an hour helping him clean up the basement and then the attic and then the garage. Even then it would probably take eight years to earn the money. And no one should have to work eight years for a bedroom set. So I'm going to work for a new sleeping bag instead."

"A bedroom set might cost even more than a piano," said Eileen, suddenly wondering what on earth she could do to earn the money for a piano.

"Maybe," said Stephanie. "Anyway, it doesn't matter. We'll make a great pair all the same."

"What doesn't matter?" said Eileen stupidly.

"Your Halloween costume, of course. The tiger and the ghost. We can creep around and pounce out at everyone." Stephanie growled like a tiger.

Eileen swallowed the lump in her throat. "I won't be going trick-or-treating with you."

"Huh?" Stephanie stopped. She took Eileen's arm. "What?"

"I think maybe I'm going somewhere with my dad on Halloween."

"But we always do Halloween together."

Eileen pulled free and kept walking.

"Where are you going with him?"

"Trick-or-treating."

"With your dad? Your dad never came before." Stephanie shook her head in confusion. "Well, there's no reason why that has to stop our going together."

Eileen kept walking.

"Listen, Eileen." Stephanie's face was pinched with worry. "Do you want me along or not?"

"Not this time," Eileen said softly. She picked up a bright red maple leaf. "Why do you think maples turn so much brighter than other trees?"

"Who cares?" said Stephanie. She walked fast now and passed Eileen.

"Maybe no one knows."

"It's the sugar," said Stephanie sharply. She stopped. "Anyone knows that. The more sugar in the sap, the brighter the colors in the fall."

"Maple syrup," said Eileen.

"Exactly."

Eileen looked up to the very top of the tall maple.

"You think maybe we could make maple syrup from that tree?"

Stephanie shook her head. "It wouldn't be worth the trouble." The angry edge in her voice was beginning to wear off. "It takes something like forty gallons of sap to make a single gallon of maple syrup."

"Wow. That's as bad as working eight years to earn a bedroom set."

"Yup," said Stephanie. "And it's ghoulish anyway. Sap is like blood to the tree. So eating maple syrup is like drinking concentrated blood. Can you imagine what the trees must think of us? They probably see us all as vampires."

"Trees don't think," said Eileen.

"You can't be sure of that," said Stephanie. "Experiments with plants show some grow better when there's music and pleasant voices. And they wither if there's shouting or fighting. So who knows whether they think."

"Stephanie." Eileen stared at the maple tree as she talked. "Steph, my folks had a sort of a fight."

"Oh." Stephanie was walking again. "Hurry up, we're going to be late."

Eileen ran to catch up. "A bad one."

"That's a bummer. My folks fight all the time. Everyone's do. It's just 'cause you've got the perfect family that it doesn't happen all the time at your house. Your mom and dad are always so polite to each other."

"The perfect family . . ." said Eileen softly. So Stephanie thought Mom and Daddy were being nice to each other all those times that they were really avoiding talking to each other. Eileen tugged at her backpack straps. "Tomorrow's Saturday. Let's spend all day together, okay?"

"You sure you want to? You just said you didn't want to spend Halloween with me."

"I can't spend Halloween with you. That's just how it is, Steph."

Stephanie looked at Eileen with worry on her face. "Okay."

"So will you be with me tomorrow?"

"Sure," said Stephanie. "What do you want to do?"

"Mom bought another one of those blueberry muffin mixes. We could bake."

"Okay," said Stephanie. "I'll bring over the family of rock butterflies I made with Suzanne and we can play with them."

"Rock butterflies?" Eileen got a crooked smile. "I mean, imagine them flying."

Stephanie got a crooked smile too. "You're right. Can you imagine what they sound like when they flap their wings?"

Eileen and Stephanie looked at each other with grins and said together, "Clunk, clunk, clunk."

four

CHOPSTICKS

*E*ileen watched the clock. In three minutes the bell would ring. Her stomach growled. At lunchtime when she opened her lunch box, she discovered that her apple had tumbled against her sandwich and squashed it. So she ate the apple and ignored the sandwich. And now she felt like she was dying of starvation. She leaned over and whispered, "Stephanie. Stephanie."

Stephanie had her desktop up and her body scrunched down under it. She worked over the open desk, humming softly to herself. From in front of the desk no one could see what she was doing—the desktop blocked all views. But from the side Eileen could see perfectly. Stephanie was putting blue polish on her fingernails.

Eileen sniffed at the sharp enamel odor. "Stephanie," she whispered as loud as she dared. Mr. Kressler stood at the front of the classroom, writing the schedule of lessons for next Monday. Eileen leaned as far as she could toward Stephanie's desk. "Steph," she hissed.

Stephanie turned her head, with the desktop still resting on it, and smiled at Eileen. "Shhh," she said. She turned her head back and went on polishing.

Eileen looked around the classroom. Every Friday at the end of the day everyone was supposed to straighten their desks and get their notes in order so that they would know what homework they had to do over the weekend. Everyone else seemed to be doing just that, except for Milo, who sat picking fluff balls off his old sweater and stuffing them into a side zipper pocket of his new red backpack. Eileen leaned across the aisle. "I'm not walking home with you today," she whispered.

Stephanie looked up with a start. The desktop banged down on her arms. "Lift it quick," she whispered.

Eileen lifted the desk top and held it open.

Stephanie surveyed her fingernails. "Not too much damage." She screwed the top on the jar of polish and put her palm against the inside of the desktop. "You can let go now."

The bell rang. "Thanks for a great week, kids," said Mr. Kressler. "Have a safe weekend."

Eileen grabbed her backpack and stood up.

"Wait," called Stephanie. She stuffed papers into her backpack and jammed her arms through the straps as she stood up. "So?"

"So what?" asked Eileen, walking down the aisle to the coat hooks at the back of the room.

"So why aren't you walking home with me?"

Eileen took a deep breath. "I'm going to the auditorium."

"The piano again?"

Eileen put her jacket on. "Yeah."

"Why? No one else has to practice in the auditorium for the Halloween Day pageant. Why do you?"

"I'm not playing in the Halloween Day pageant," said Eileen.

"Huh? Why'd you tell me you were?"

"I never said I was. You said."

Stephanie followed Eileen out into the hall. "So why are you going to the auditorium?"

"I told you," Eileen said.

"You didn't tell me," Stephanie said. "You forget to tell me lots of things."

"I told you yesterday," said Eileen.

"Yesterday doesn't count."

Eileen walked more slowly. This was the moment to tell Stephanie. Now, right here in the hall. How should she start?

Stephanie grabbed Eileen's jacket sleeve and stopped still. "You haven't said anything about my nails."

Eileen looked at Stephanie's nails. "Why blue?"

"It's more tigerlike."

Eileen scratched her neck. "Tigers don't have blue nails."

"I know." Stephanie curled her fingers like claws. "They have black nails. Only I don't have any black polish. And at night in the dark, blue will look like black."

"At night in the dark every color looks like black."

Stephanie put her hands behind her back. "You work too hard. Forget practicing on the auditorium piano. Walk home with me instead."

"I like it," lied Eileen. She looked down. "Better tie your laces. I'll call you about tomorrow. Blueberry muffins. Don't forget."

"I won't forget," said Stephanie. "Don't you forget."

The auditorium was as dark as yesterday, but it didn't seem quite as big today. Eileen pushed in the bench and sat down. She spread out her music and stared at it until her eyes focused enough to see the notes. This was annoying, practicing in the dark. And it was probably bad for her eyes. She'd probably need glasses by the end of the year. That's what this ugly piano was doing to her—making her wrists weak and ruining her eyes. A rush of heat went up her cheeks. She hated this piano. She pursed her lips and banged out "Chopsticks" as loud as she could. Then she let her hands fall into her lap. She shuddered.

"Playing in the dark?"

Eileen pivoted around on the bench in alarm.

A man came in the side door. It was Mr. Poole, the custodian. He leaned his broom against the wall, then walked up to the steps at the side of the stage and switched on the lights near Eileen. "This is the switch you want," he said, pointing.

Eileen hardly knew Mr. Poole. "Did you hear me?" She twisted her hands.

"Sounded like 'Chopsticks' to me. They told me you were going to practice. I didn't know that meant 'Chopsticks.' " Mr. Poole smiled.

Was Mr. Poole like Mom? Did he think "Chopsticks" was a waste of time? Well, if Eileen had to play on this awful piano, she was going to play whatever she wanted. She banged out a few more bars and stopped. She looked at Mr. Poole defiantly.

"What else do you like to play?" Mr. Poole picked trash paper off the floor and carried it to the wastebasket over by the door.

Suddenly Eileen felt foolish because, in fact, she hardly ever played "Chopsticks." She didn't even like that tune. "I don't know," she half mumbled.

Mr. Poole rubbed his chin.

Eileen tapped her hands on her thighs in impatience. She didn't feel like playing anything at all anymore.

"All right, then," said Mr. Poole. "How about 'When the Saints Go Marching In'?"

If he thought she couldn't play that, he was wrong. Eileen played. It had been a long time since she'd played that song. She had forgotten some of it. She stopped in the middle of the first refrain.

Mr. Poole came over. "May I?" He leaned forward and put his hands to the keys. The skin on his arms was loose and jiggly, and he smelled of the disinfectant he used to wash the floors. Eileen wrinkled her nose and scooted to the end of the bench. Mr. Poole took a minute to position his hands. Then he picked up where she had left off and finished it. It wasn't precise, and it wasn't like Eileen used to play it. But it was vibrant and confident, and Eileen loved the way each refrain differed a little from the last. It was wonderful.

The music filled the auditorium. Eileen waited for it to die down. "That was good," she said at last.

"Thank you," said Mr. Poole, standing straight and letting his arms fall to his sides.

"I messed it up," Eileen said apologetically. "I forgot it because I haven't played it in so long."

"Ah, but that isn't all you play."

Eileen's heart jumped. "Did you hear me yesterday?"

"A bit. One of those tunes you played was sweet and smooth."

Smooth? "The piano sounded terrible."

"No it didn't."

"The keys bounce back too fast," said Eileen.

"That just shows this piano recognizes a superior player." Mr. Poole leaned forward again and ran his hand across the keyboard. "Yup, you made this girl come alive."

Eileen looked at the scuffed-up wood of the piano in surprise. "It's so old."

"That's right." Mr. Poole let out a low, appreciative whistle. He smiled. "Did you know these keys are real ivory?"

Eileen rubbed a key. Had an elephant really died just to make these keys? Last year her class had talked about animal poaching in Africa as part of their ecology and the environment section in science. "There are laws against killing elephants."

"This piano was built long before those laws. The maker was thinking only about beauty. Real ivory keys. That's why they're yellow. The fake ivory on new pianos never yellows." Mr. Poole turned and went to the front row of the auditorium. He sat down. "Will you play me that sweet tune from yesterday?"

Eileen opened her Burgmüller book slowly and sat up tall. She wished she was alone again, but she had to act polite. She played loud and clear.

"That's good, little lady. That's terrific." Mr. Poole got up. "Tell me, what's your name?"

"Eileen."

"I'll sweep while you play, Eileen, okay?"

Eileen played. She went from one book to the next. She played and played, without letting her eyes stray from the notes on the page. Finally, she checked her watch. It had been a good forty-five minutes. She closed up her books and looked around. Mr. Poole had disappeared, but he'd left his broom behind, so he was clearly planning on returning. In a way, Eileen wanted to say good-bye to him. But it seemed silly to wait. And, anyway, maybe he hadn't been around for most of her playing. Maybe he'd just been sweeping. Maybe he hadn't listened at all.

But maybe he had.

She walked out of the auditorium and straight to the bench on the school playground. She opened her backpack and reached in for the squished sandwich. It smelled wonderful. Tuna fish. She ate it. Then she ran home, carrying her backpack by the little loop at the top. It bumped against her left leg in even beats. The air was cold and crisp.

five

BIG CHANGES

*E*ileen." Mrs. Tilly stood in her doorway, beckoning. "Do you want to come in? I'd like you to meet someone."

Eileen veered off the sidewalk with a smile and followed Mrs. Tilly into the house. "Oh," she breathed, catching sight of the stranger right away, "oh, who's that?" She dropped her backpack and walked over to the little wooden cradle on the floor in the living room. She knelt beside it.

The baby looked at Eileen with big brown unblinking eyes.

"Don't you love him?" Mrs. Tilly leaned across Eileen's

shoulder and crooned. "Isn't he the best little baby in the world?"

"Can I hold him?"

Mrs. Tilly put one hand under the baby's head from one side and the other hand under the baby's bottom from the other side and lifted him out of the cradle. She placed him gently in Eileen's arms. Eileen was careful to keep the crook of her left arm under the baby's neck and to hold tight with her right arm. She had held babies before. She backed into the couch and sat in the corner so that the couch's side gave extra support. Mrs. Tilly sat near her.

"What's his name?"

"Jared."

"That's a good name," said Eileen happily. "Whose baby is he?"

Mrs. Tilly sat up a little taller. "He's my grandson."

"Oh. The last time I saw Kit she was thin. I didn't even know she was pregnant."

"She wasn't." Mrs. Tilly stood up and smiled serenely. "Jared's adopted. It's a big change all of a sudden. A wonderful change. How about a snack today?"

Eileen shook her head. "I just ate my lunch sandwich."

"Maybe cookies, then?" Mrs. Tilly hurried out to the kitchen, humming contentedly.

Eileen looked at Jared. Jared squirmed. He was swaddled in a yellow blanket. Eileen unwrapped him slowly. Jared flailed his arms. He wore pajamas that covered his feet and hands entirely. Eileen peeled back one mitten of the pajamas and held Jared's small hand in hers. Jared's fingers moved open and closed and open and closed and finally curled around Eileen's index finger. "I'm Eileen. I'm your neighbor. Your grandmother's neighbor, that is. And I'm going to see you a lot." She pulled her finger loose and ran her hand across Jared's fuzzy head.

"Ahhh," sighed Jared, gazing at her. He smiled.

"He smiled," Eileen called out. "He smiled at me, Mrs. Tilly."

Mrs. Tilly came into the living room and set a plate of cookies on the coffee table. "Of course he did. He's already four and a half months old. He's very friendly." Mrs. Tilly reached for Jared. "Let me take him while you eat." Eileen handed Jared to Mrs. Tilly, and he grabbed the old woman's glasses.

Eileen took a bite of a cookie. "Thank you."

Mrs. Tilly swaddled Jared tight again.

"I think he likes being loose," said Eileen. "He didn't smile at me until I unwrapped him."

Mrs. Tilly looked at Eileen thoughtfully. "All right. It will be harder for me that way, but it might be more fun for him." Mrs. Tilly unwrapped Jared and spread the blanket on the rug. Then she set Jared on his back in the middle of the blanket. Jared smiled. Mrs. Tilly laughed.

"Oh." Eileen stood up quickly. "I better go tell my mother where I am."

"She isn't home."

Mom wasn't home? Eileen's stomach lurched. "Where is she?"

"At a job interview."

And if Mom got this job, was she going to be gone every day when Eileen got home from school? Eileen felt a tug of loneliness. Almost abandonment. But that was silly. She didn't need Mom home. She didn't even care where Mom was.

Jared kicked his legs into the air and grabbed his feet.

Eileen got down on the rug beside him. "Here." She took a foot in each hand and did patty-cake with Jared's feet. Jared smiled.

"You're very good with him," said Mrs. Tilly. "I'm

afraid I'm getting too old to be taking care of a baby. I'm sixty-six already. And Kit's almost forty."

Forty. Eileen's mother wasn't anywhere near forty yet. "Why did Kit wait so long to get a baby?"

"She and Jim were hoping to have one of their own. But some things are outside your control."

Eileen looked down at the baby on the blanket. "And now she has Jared. She's lucky."

"Yes," said Mrs. Tilly, "we all are."

Friday night Eileen sat reading, curled in the blue lumpy chair in her room, listening to the rain splat against her window. The whine of the sewing machine surprised her. She closed her book and walked down the stairs to the little sewing room off the kitchen.

"Eileen." Mom looked up, startled. She was flushed. "I thought you were asleep." Spotted furry material covered the narrow sewing table. Mom sighed. "I should have known I couldn't keep a secret from you."

"What are you making?"

"Stephanie's mother lent me a cat suit pattern. She made Stephanie a tiger costume for Halloween. I thought you might like to be a leopard."

Eileen rubbed the furry material and stood close to

her mother. "I wish I could wear it with Stephanie. I wish I could go trick-or-treating with her. I wish . . ."

Mom slipped her arm loosely around Eileen's waist. "What do you wish, Eileen?"

"I wish everything was like it used to be."

"Things will never be like they used to be." Mom turned off the tiny sewing machine light and pushed her chair back. She pulled Eileen gently onto her lap. "Changes are often hard to get used to. But they can be good. You and I will find ways to enjoy being us. Special together. And when you're at Daddy's home, you'll be special with him."

"I miss us being all three." Eileen touched the pearly buttons on her mother's blouse.

Mom nodded. "Do you know Mrs. Wellington, Eileen?"

Eileen shook her head.

"She's the school psychologist. She likes to talk to children when their families are having problems."

Eileen stood up. "I don't want to talk to her."

"Sometimes it helps to talk about your pr___ ___."

"You and Daddy are the ones who shoul__ ___ __ ___"

"Eileen." Mom folded her hands in her lap. "We're talking about you right now—about getting you help in accepting all these changes—not about Daddy and me."

six

MUFFINS

Saturday's sunshine warmed the kitchen.

"Want to add chocolate chips on top? You know, in a happy face or something?" Stephanie licked the muffin batter off her fingers.

"I don't think chocolate chips go great with blueberries," said Eileen doubtfully.

"Chocolate chips go great with anything," said Stephanie. "But if you have to be picky about it, we could use raisins."

Eileen wrinkled her nose. She went to the cupboard and came back with three boxes. "Spaghetti, elbow noodles, and little stars. We can break the spaghetti into any lengths we need."

Stephanie giggled. "Did you know that there are dozens of types of pasta? My cousin has a pasta poster on her bedroom wall. I don't mean a poster made of pasta. I mean a poster about pasta."

Eileen arranged elbow noodles into a pattern on a muffin top and nodded slightly to Stephanie to go on.

Stephanie didn't notice. She went right on anyway. "There are pasta shaped like snails and scallops and springs and tubes and everything. And each different shape has its own kind of taste, even though they're all made of the same dough. And—"

"I don't see how," said Eileen.

"You don't see how what?"

"I don't see how different shapes of the same dough can taste different." Eileen finished off the decorations on her third muffin.

"Well, they do."

"How do you know?"

"Everyone says so."

Eileen turned on the oven. She decorated another muffin. "Are you done?"

Stephanie looked at her muffins. She had been talking

so much, she hadn't even begun to decorate her half of the pan. "Help me."

Together the girls finished off the pan. Then Eileen put it in the oven and set the timer for twelve minutes.

"Now what?" said Stephanie.

"I guess we should clean up." Eileen filled half the sink with soapy water and washed the bowl and measuring cup and stirring spoon while Stephanie wiped off the table and cleaned up the spills on the floor. Then Eileen sat beside Stephanie at the table in silence. Eileen couldn't remember having sat in silence with Stephanie ever before. She looked at the timer. Three more minutes to go. Eileen counted the seconds inside her head.

The timer dinged.

Eileen took the pot holders and pulled the pan out of the oven. She set the pan on the counter to cool and shut off the oven. "Want one while they're still hot?"

"Look." Stephanie inspected the muffins with a critical expression on her face. "The pasta turned brown."

"It probably tastes the same," said Eileen with a laugh. "Want to meet Jared?"

"Who's Jared? There's a new kid around and I didn't know it? I'm always the one to welcome new people. After all, I'm the one who introduced Mandy to everyone when she moved here last year, even though she isn't our friend anymore. I bet she's decorating for that party right now. Maybe if we showed up at her doorstep tonight with these muffins in our hands, she'd invite us in to the party."

Eileen shook her head. "You don't really like her that much, anyway. Admit it."

"It's not a question of who likes who. It's a question of a party. There's a party tonight, and we aren't invited."

Eileen felt a wicked giggle coming on. "What happened to all that talk about it's better not getting everything you want?"

Stephanie looked at Eileen and grinned. "Okay. So we're better off. Come on, tell me. Who is Jared?"

"Come see." Eileen walked out the kitchen door, with Stephanie close at her heels. She skirted around the puddles from last night's downpour, went to the front of Mrs. Tilly's house, and rang the bell.

"Did that old lady move away?" whispered Stephanie.

"Her name's Mrs. Tilly." Eileen rang again.

The door opened. "Well, hello, Eileen. And here's your friend Stephanie. That's right, isn't it, your name is Stephanie?"

"Yes." Stephanie smiled politely.

"Would you like to come in, girls?" Mrs. Tilly stood back.

Eileen tried to look past Mrs. Tilly into the living room. "Is Jared here?"

"Is that who you came to see? No, little Jared is with his mother today. I only get him in the afternoons on Monday through Friday, when Kit goes in to work." Mrs. Tilly opened the door wider. "Come in."

"We really shouldn't," said Eileen.

"Well, of course you girls have lots of other things to do," said Mrs. Tilly. "Come back later if you like."

Eileen backed down off the porch steps. "See you Monday afternoon, okay?"

"That's a fine idea." Mrs. Tilly waved and shut the door.

Stephanie took Eileen by the arm and dragged her across the grass. "Who's Jared?"

"Mrs. Tilly's grandson. A baby."

"Oooo," said Stephanie. "I love babies. I even know how to diaper them. My sister took me baby-sitting once this summer, and she let me change the kid's diapers. It's easy if all they do is pee. And then it's not so yucky. Can I come home with you on Monday to meet him?"

"Not Monday," Eileen said in a flat voice.

Stephanie let go of Eileen's arm. "You know, I don't

see why we see each other at all anymore. It seems like you don't even like me these days."

"What?" said Eileen. "We're best friends."

"Suzanne invites me over more than you do." Stephanie stamped through a puddle.

"You can come home with me on Monday," said Eileen. She could skip practice one day. What difference would it make?

"Really?" said Stephanie.

"Really," said Eileen.

"Okay." Stephanie ran through the puddles toward Eileen's back door. Then she stopped. "I forgot. I have an appointment on Monday."

"And we have piano lesson on Tuesday," said Eileen. "Okay, then, come on Wednesday."

Stephanie gave a sheepish smile. "Suzanne is coming to my house on Wednesday."

Eileen thought of Suzanne and Stephanie making rock butterflies together. On Wednesday maybe they'd move on to rock dragonflies. Then rock ladybugs. A whole rock insect zoo. Eileen picked up an oak leaf. "We can figure out a day later on." She crumpled the leaf. It was yellow, spotted with brown. The spots reminded her. "Come see what my mother is making."

"What is it?"

"A leopard costume."

"For Halloween." Stephanie giggled. "Does this mean you've changed your mind and you'll go trick-or-treating with me?"

"I can't, Steph."

Stephanie folded her arms across her chest. "So what do I care if you'll be a leopard? It makes no difference to me."

"We could dress up together."

"When?"

"Anytime."

Stephanie looked thoughtful. "Well, I guess so." She smiled slowly. "We can be stalking cats together. Grrr," growled Stephanie.

"Sssss," hissed Eileen.

seven

FAKES

*E*ileen entered the auditorium. She breathed in the dusty air. The place felt familiar to her now, even in the dark. She had come every day this week after school except Tuesday. On Tuesday she had gone with Stephanie to Mr. Gilbert's house for piano lessons. It was now Thursday, and Eileen was accustomed to the routine. She walked confidently down the center aisle and spread out her music sheets. Then she shut her eyes and played her scales.

Scales didn't have to be played with shut eyes, and Eileen never used to play them that way. But it had become a sort of game. And it was easy once she got used to it. In fact, it was so easy that Eileen wanted a bigger challenge. She had studied her exercise book at home and practiced with her fingers drumming on her desk. If she could memorize the exercises for each week, then she could play them with shut eyes too. But so far Eileen's attempts at playing the exercises with shut eyes hadn't been too successful.

But the scales sounded nice. Eileen had long slender fingers like her father, and even last year in fourth grade she didn't have to grope for keys the way Stephanie still did with her short fingers. Eileen hit each key with precision.

Tomorrow Eileen would go to her father's place for the weekend. They would take walks and eat pizza and go trick-or-treating and skip church and Sunday school and read comics and pretend they were on some sort of vacation instead of starting a new kind of life. And Eileen could practice on her familiar piano again. Or, better, maybe she could convince her father to play something with her.

Or maybe she'd pretend the piano wasn't there. Maybe that would show her father that it didn't matter if he had taken the piano. She didn't care anyway. He could play all by himself, all alone in his own place without Mom or Eileen to bother him.

A weekend full of pretending. A fake daughter and a fake father.

Eileen squeezed her eyes shut even harder. Her fingers moved faster and faster. She was getting used to the quick action of this keyboard.

This piano might be ugly and old, but it was no fake.

Eileen played softer and slower. Her muscles loosened. Her breath came easily. She played smoothly.

Midway through the third scale, the lights clicked on. Eileen opened her eyes. She looked up and laughed.

Mr. Poole stood at the steps by the stage and smiled back at her. This was part of the game. Eileen always played in the dark until Mr. Poole turned on the lights. He walked over to the first row and took a seat. "Those scales are getting better and better, but I bet you're straining those eyes."

Eileen giggled. "I keep my eyes closed."

"I thought maybe something like that was going on." Mr. Poole slid down till his neck hit the back of the wooden seat. "Let me hear a smooth tune."

"Not today."

"What?" Mr. Poole sat up straight. "You always start with a smooth tune."

"I want to play something different today. It's jazzy."

"Hmm. Well, then, I guess I'll do my work. I like to keep moving when I hear jazz." Mr. Poole leaned forward and picked up a crushed juice box off the floor, as if to make his point. He stuck it halfway into his back pocket. Then he took his broom and went up the aisle, sweeping carefully.

Eileen did a few extra scales and exercises, just to make sure she was ready. Finally, she opened the book of Joplin arrangements to "Maple Leaf Rag." It was the first time she'd opened to that page since she'd been coming to the auditorium to play. She hesitated.

This was the piece she had planned to surprise Daddy with. But the motivation for surprising him had broken down when Daddy took the piano. It was almost as though she had kept away from Joplin's music to punish Daddy—which didn't make sense, of course, since Daddy didn't even know she had planned to play this music.

But she wasn't going to stay away from it anymore. Eileen liked Scott Joplin all on her own, not just because Daddy played him. And of all the Joplin tunes she knew, she liked "Maple Leaf Rag" best. So Daddy didn't matter. This tune was for Eileen.

She played the right hand alone, then the left alone,

then both together. The right hand made use of half beats—and-one-and-two-and-three-and-four. And the left hand used only one-two-three-four. It wouldn't be so hard to put them together if they both started each measure on the same count, but they didn't. Almost every other measure, the right hand would rest for the first half beat. Eileen divided the piece into four fairly equal parts and worked on only the first part. She counted under her breath. She played it again and again. She let her body move a little—lean into the keys, her shoulders rising and falling.

"Yes, that's it," said Mr. Poole.

Eileen gave a little gasp; Mr. Poole's voice came to her as if out of a dream. She had completely forgotten he was in the auditorium.

"Yup. You're into it now."

She smiled; Mr. Poole was right. Moving her body helped get her inside the music. She finished the last measure of this section. Working on new material was always hard, even though it was exciting. She deserved a break now. She took out an old Chopin prelude she hadn't played for a while and played it straight through without any mistakes, the very first time. She played it a second time. And a third. Maybe her ears were fooling her, but it sounded better here than it ever had at home. Sadder, more piercing. She finished and looked around for Mr. Poole.

"You done already?" Mr. Poole had just finished sweeping the audience area. He carried his broom up onto the stage.

Eileen watched him work for a while. "Will you come listen to me tomorrow?"

"Sure will."

Eileen hesitated. It seemed silly to ask, because he'd been listening to her ever since last week. But somehow she wanted to know for sure. She blurted out, "Will you come every day? Except Tuesday. On Tuesday I go right to my piano lesson after school."

"So that's where you were on Tuesday." Mr. Poole moved the podium from the center of the stage, back to the side where it normally stood. "Every day but Tuesday, then."

Eileen closed her music books. "Which piece did you like better, the Joplin or the Chopin?"

"The Chopin was that last bit, huh?"

"Yes." Eileen almost added "of course," but she stopped herself. Could Mr. Poole really not recognize Chopin?

"I have to admit it, Eileen, that Chopin leaves me wondering."

"What do you mean?"

"I don't know. It didn't feel like it ended." Mr. Poole shrugged. "You played it pretty, though."

Eileen flipped through the music books in her pack. "What sort of music do you like to play?"

"Me?" Mr. Poole chuckled. "I can't play."

"Come on." Eileen scooted to one side to make room on the bench. "I've got five books here. Some of the songs are great. Please play for me."

"But I can't, Eileen." Mr. Poole walked over to the bench and looked over Eileen's shoulder at the books. He picked out the new Beethoven book that Mom had bought when she discovered Eileen's old Beethoven book had disappeared. He opened it. "Hmmmm. Beethoven. Now everyone's heard of him. 'Moonlight Sonata.' Can you play this?"

"No." Mr. Gilbert had never assigned her that, thank heavens. It sort of bored her with those slow, heavy notes. "My father plays it a lot." Eileen wondered if she should say "played." After all, maybe he didn't play it a lot these days. She wouldn't know. She didn't live with him these days. "But I bet you can play it even better," she said belligerently.

Mr. Poole guffawed. "What gives you that idea?"

"I heard you."

"You mean with 'The Saints'? That's all I play."

Eileen shook her head in confusion. "What do you mean?"

"That's all I know. I never had a piano. Are you kidding? Who could afford such a thing? I learned 'The Saints' by heart from the minister of our church when I was ten years old. Just about your age, right? How old are you?"

Eileen's cheeks got hot. She felt dizzy. "Ten."

Mr. Poole chuckled. "Yup. I was just like you. I used to go to the church every day after school. Like you come to this auditorium. And Minister Hayes taught me. He showed me note by note and . . ."

Eileen wasn't listening anymore. Mr. Poole didn't know how to play the piano. He knew one song by heart. That's all. Of course. Mr. Poole was a school custodian. And he was poor as a child. Poor people don't have pianos. Eileen wasn't even really poor, and still she and her mother couldn't afford to just go out and buy a piano. How stupid could Eileen be? Really poor people can't even afford lessons. Really poor people have to hang around the church, like Mr. Poole did, or the school, or someplace public and sneak onto some beaten-up old piano when no one was around and sort of diddle their fingers hopefully.

Here was Eileen, who used to have a piano and would again someday, she knew she would someday, and who still had lessons once a week, and she had done something stupid that made it obvious how poor Mr. Poole was compared to her.

"No. I can play one thing," Mr. Poole said with a nod, "and you've heard it already."

Eileen blinked and looked down. She'd rather die than cry now. Mr. Poole mustn't understand how she felt.

"Oh, now, Eileen." Mr. Poole's voice was gentle and low. "Is something the matter? Why, you're disappointed in me. Well, I'll be. You got the wrong impression."

Eileen looked up at Mr. Poole. His face was as sad as she felt.

Mr. Poole shook his head. "I didn't mean to disappoint you."

"No," said Eileen quickly, "you didn't. I just feel stupid."

Mr. Poole stepped back with amazement on his face. "You? You're clever, Eileen. I can tell that from listening to you play." Mr. Poole tilted his head. "So your father plays this here Beethoven?"

"He's good at the piano."

"Must run in the genes," said Mr. Poole.

"He told me once that when he was younger, he wanted to be a concert pianist. He wasn't good enough, though."

"Maybe you'll be the professional pianist of the family."

Eileen shook her head. "If Daddy wasn't good enough, I'll never be."

"Who says? You might wind up playing in a nightclub. You never know." Mr. Poole put the Beethoven book on the stack of music books. He picked up his broom. "If you're done for today, I'm off to the cafeteria. See you tomorrow."

eight

GREEN

*E*ileen turned on to the stone path up to Mrs. Tilly's house.

"Boo!" Stephanie jumped out from behind the hedge.

Eileen's mouth opened in dismay. "What are you doing here?"

"What kind of welcome is that?" Stephanie put both hands on her hips. "You jumped out at me last week. Now it was my turn. Aren't you surprised? Aren't you glad to see me?"

Almost any other time Eileen would have been overjoyed to find Stephanie waiting for her. But not now. Eileen had walked home from the auditorium thinking about how good it was to have Mr. Poole listen to her practice. At the same time she was still sad to realize he didn't play the piano. From just that one time when he had played "When the Saints Go Marching In" she knew that he loved the piano. He probably said that about playing a piano in a nightclub because that's what he wished he could do. But he'd never had the chance. He couldn't control what family he was born into.

Just like Eileen couldn't control what family she was born into.

A lot in life was beyond control. And that realization made Eileen feel tired. So right now she wanted nothing more than simply to sit on Mrs. Tilly's rug with Jared on the floor beside her and gaze into those big, innocent, baby eyes. Eileen could make Jared laugh no matter how sad Eileen felt. And when Jared laughed, Eileen laughed.

"Hey, are you there?" Stephanie moved her face closer to Eileen's with a look of concern. "You know, sometimes I just don't understand you, Eileen. These days you seem to walk around in a dream. You hardly say anything anymore. I have to do all the talking. And I like talking, but now and then you have to talk too. Come on. Wake up."

Stephanie's words hit like little sharp pings; they left a sting. Eileen tried to smile past them.

Stephanie smiled back. "Well, good. I'm here and I'm ready to play. Aren't you at least a little bit glad to see me?"

Eileen forced herself to look friendly. "Yeah, but I can't play now. I promised Mrs. Tilly I'd help with Jared." Eileen started to walk past Stephanie.

Stephanie didn't budge. "Listen, Eileen, you tell me all these wonderful things about Jared every day, and I've never even seen him." Stephanie stepped beside Eileen and hooked her arm through Eileen's. "Let me come with you. The way society is changing, we'll probably be in our thirties before we have a baby of our own. And maybe we'll never have babies. Some women don't. Especially ones who want careers. Lots of serious women don't have babies. I love to play with babies. So let me come with you and see Jared. Please." They stood now in front of Mrs. Tilly's door. Stephanie put her finger up to the bell and held it poised in midair. "Please, Eileen. I'd share a baby with you if I knew one."

All that stuff about careers and being thirty meant nothing to Eileen. It was too far away. But Stephanie was right. Eileen knew that Stephanie would share a baby with Eileen if Stephanie knew one. Eileen nodded silently.

Stephanie rang the bell. "Thank you," she whispered ecstatically. "Thank you so much."

"Well, hello, young ladies. It's nice to see you again, Stephanie." Mrs. Tilly held Jared in her arms facing outward. Jared's mouth hung open, and a thread of drool dangled from the side of his tongue. He stared at Stephanie. "You're a bit earlier than usual today, aren't you, Eileen dear? I've been working on something in the kitchen, but I'm afraid Jared has slowed me down. I'm so glad you're here now."

Eileen and Stephanie went into the house and put their backpacks and jackets on the radiator cover under the window. Eileen reached for Jared. "Here, let me take him while you go cook."

At the sound of Eileen's voice, Jared took his eyes off Stephanie and flailed his arms. He gave an openmouthed smile and let out a squeal of delight.

"He likes you," said Stephanie. "He likes you a lot, Eileen."

Eileen took Jared and walked into the living room. She lay Jared on the rug and spread out his blanket. Then she placed Jared on the center of the blanket like she always did. "Hello, little funny face. How are you today?" She got on her hands and knees and nuzzled Jared's tummy.

Jared giggled and grabbed Eileen's hair with both hands. "Ouch. Help me, Steph."

Stephanie and Eileen unfolded Jared's fingers gently till Eileen was free. Jared grabbed Stephanie's finger and held fast. Stephanie laughed.

Jared stared at her.

"You certainly have big eyes, don't you? And a strong grip. Maybe you're going to be an athlete. You could even become a wrestler. Not a sumo wrestler, you'll never be that obese, I hope. But some other kind." Stephanie laughed and jiggled Jared's hand.

Jared stared.

"You can come out onto the wrestling mat and you'll be so impressive, the referee will blow a bugle to announce you. Ba ba ba baaa ba-baaa." Stephanie lifted her chin as she imitated a bugle.

Jared let go of Stephanie's finger and cried.

"She scared you, poor baby." Eileen picked up Jared and cuddled him, half laughing. "You poor funny little dink. Stephanie would never hurt you. She was just being a bugle."

Jared stopped crying and held close to Eileen.

Stephanie sat back on her heels with an apologetic

look. "I guess I have to make friends with you slowly, Jared. I sort of took it for granted that you'd understand me. But of course you didn't. And you shouldn't have." Stephanie walked on her knees across the blanket.

Jared looked at her apprehensively from the circle of Eileen's arms.

"It takes time to get to know people." Stephanie smiled encouragingly. Her voice was as warm as melting butter. "I'll be more quiet now, I promise." Stephanie sidled closer. "Won't you try again with me, Jared?" She held out her hand.

Eileen took Jared's little hand and stretched it out to touch Stephanie's hand.

Jared stared at Stephanie.

"He'll get used to you." Eileen tried to lay Jared back on the blanket, but Jared clung to her. So Eileen crossed her ankles and propped Jared in the little well made by her legs. "Let's sing. He loves songs."

Eileen and Stephanie sang "Home on the Range" and "Yankee Doodle."

"Well, now, that's cheerful." Mrs. Tilly set a tray on the coffee table in front of the couch. "Here, let me take Jared while you girls have a snack."

Eileen handed Jared to Mrs. Tilly as she looked forward eagerly to the snack on the coffee table. She sniffed the air, taking in the sweet pungent odor.

The smell was great, but the sight wasn't. A green loaf sat on a cutting board. Eileen moved closer and inspected.

Stephanie leaned across Eileen's shoulder and whispered, "Why is it green?"

Eileen shrugged. Then she cleared her throat. "What is this?" she asked as politely as she could.

"Zucchini bread," said Mrs. Tilly gaily.

"Zucchini's a vegetable," Stephanie announced, stepping back from the table.

Mrs. Tilly smiled proudly at the loaf. "It's easy. And good for you too."

Stephanie nodded slowly.

Eileen suppressed a sigh of doubt. She looked at the green bread. The color was just unusual, that's all.

"Dig in, girls."

Eileen looked at Stephanie. Stephanie looked back. Eileen reached for the knife and cut herself a small slice. She took a bite and smiled.

"Do you like it?" asked Mrs. Tilly.

"Mmmhmmm," Eileen mumbled as she chewed. She looked at Jared, whose mouth hung open again. As Eileen took another bite, Jared pushed his fist into his mouth. "Do you think Jared wants a taste?"

"He's too small for solid food yet. But I hope someday he'll love my snacks. I want to be a good grandmother."

"You're a wonderful grandmother, Mrs. Tilly."

"Why, thank you, Eileen. Won't you have a slice too, Stephanie?"

"No, thank you." Stephanie looked around the room. "I'm not really hungry. Anyway, we eat dinner early, and my mom doesn't like it if I ruin my appetite." Stephanie talked a little faster now. Eileen could see she was warming up. "My sister says that you should never eat when you're not hungry because then you'll get in the habit and you'll get fat. People have to listen hard to their bodies and eat only when their bodies tell them to. Being hungry is the body's way of saying, 'Feed me.' And your metabolism is ready to burn up the food when you're hungry. But if you eat when you're not hungry, it all turns into fat and sits in your thighs."

Mrs. Tilly looked at Stephanie with amazement.

Eileen tried to hold in her laugh and failed. Crumbs of

zucchini bread flew everywhere. "I'm sorry," she muttered, and she laughed again.

"It's true," said Stephanie. "Why are you laughing?"

"It sits in your thighs." Eileen laughed louder now.

"That's what my sister says."

"It sounds right to me," said Mrs. Tilly. "If you're not hungry, Stephanie, let's not ruin your thighs." She smiled. "Sometimes a molasses cookie can rouse the appetite of someone who has just a very small appetite. I believe I have one thin molasses cookie left. Molasses cookies never make thighs heavy. Would you like it?"

"Thank you," said Stephanie in a formal voice. "That sounds fabulous."

Mrs. Tilly put Jared on the blanket and went to the kitchen.

"Are you glad you came?" asked Eileen.

"Sure," said Stephanie determinedly. "Mrs. Tilly's a little bit weird. But she's nice too. And Jared's great." Stephanie knelt down beside Jared. Jared gave her a small smile. Stephanie grinned from ear to ear.

nine

NEW MUSIC

"Three cereal bowls is all you have?" Eileen stood in front of the open cupboard with disgust on her face. The shelves were close to bare. Eileen looked over her shoulder at Daddy. "Three bowls."

"Three's all I need." Daddy sat at the kitchen counter on a stool and watched Eileen with a contented look on his face. The emptiness of his cupboards didn't seem to bother him.

Eileen took the bowls with a sigh of resignation and set them in a row on the counter in front of Daddy. "How do you figure three?"

"One for me. One for you. One for good measure."

"Is good measure a person?"

Daddy's smile faded. "Good measure is in case there's a guest, whether it be a stray cat or a friend."

Eileen's heart beat hard. She felt skinny and small. So skinny that maybe her heartbeat showed on the outside. She looked down at her chest. It looked normal. She wouldn't ask, she wouldn't, but the words came out on their own. "A woman friend?"

Daddy pushed the three bowls together so each one touched the other two. "I told you, Eileen. I didn't leave because of another woman. I left because your mother and I can't live together anymore."

Eileen set the bowls back in a row. The counter was the only divider between the kitchen and the living room, and for just one brief moment she allowed herself to look beyond Daddy at the piano. Messy piles of sheet music covered the top. Eileen blinked and looked at Daddy. He was watching her.

She quickly opened the Halloween bag that sat on the stool beside Daddy's and looked at the jumble of candies. Tootsie Rolls and Hershey's kisses and Life Savers lollipops. Some cookies that had already crumbled. A bag of popcorn. Tons of junk.

"Aren't you going to say anything?" Daddy folded his hands together on the counter.

"How am I supposed to separate out all this candy with just three measly bowls?"

Daddy let out a low laugh. "That's not what I meant, and you know it."

Eileen looked up defiantly. "What am I supposed to say?"

Daddy's hands seemed made of steel; not a finger moved. "Maybe you could say, 'Okay.' "

"Okay," said Eileen woodenly.

"There are things you don't understand, Eileen."

"I said okay."

Daddy stuck his lips out like a fish. He always did that when he was holding back anger. "What are you separating them for?"

"Christmas, of course. The candy village."

"Oh, yeah."

A new stab of apprehension made Eileen almost gasp from pain. "Will you make it with Mom and me, like always? Will you come home long enough to do that?" Her voice sounded strange to her as she forced out the words—almost as though someone else was saying them.

"Of course I will." Daddy looked over Eileen's shoulder into the bag. "All those candy corns make nice shingles on the gingerbread houses. And the spearmint leaves are good fat little bushes. And these here"—Daddy picked up a roll of Smarties—"these make perfect wheels on the Snickers train cars. I like working on that village." Daddy looked pensive for a moment. "So all you need to do is make two piles, Eileen. One to eat now and one to stash away."

"I thought I'd separate out the candy you like, the candy Mom likes, the candy I like, and then the junk for the candy village."

Daddy got off the stool and went to the refrigerator. He took down a package of sandwich bags from off the top. "You could use these." He reached into the Halloween candy bag and took out a handful. "I like Tootsie Rolls."

"I know. And we all like anything Hershey's, so I'll divide those up fairly." Eileen's hands moved deftly through the candy. "And Mom gets all the licorice."

Daddy put back his handful of candy and watched Eileen work. "Looks like you know what you're doing. Maybe I'll relax a little." He walked across the small living room.

Eileen could see his every move. Daddy sat down at

the piano. Eileen waited with anticipation. Would it be Beethoven or jazz? What kind of mood was Daddy in? Eileen bet Beethoven. Daddy could say he wanted to relax, but Eileen knew better. He was tense, and he needed to pound out something.

Daddy played. Eileen had been wrong—it was something strange. It wasn't something she knew at all. Daddy had moved on to new music.

She left the kitchen and came over to the makeshift bookcase of boards on bricks that held all of Daddy's books. She stood with her back to the books and watched him. He was playing from memory, as though he'd known this music all his life. But he'd been gone less than a month. He sure learned this piece fast. Eileen silently willed Daddy to make a mistake. He had no right to move on to new music so fast, so easily, and just leave her behind. Let him mess up and play all the wrong notes and cry. That was it—he should be the one to cry, not Eileen. He was the one who had done something wrong.

Daddy finished. "Do you like it?"

"It's okay."

"Only okay?"

Eileen's voice took on an icy edge. "You love this piano, don't you?"

"This was my big purchase when I got my first job. I'd wanted a piano since I was a kid, and I finally had enough money. I've told you that story before. It's my buddy." Daddy folded his hand over the edge of the piano bench and held tight for a moment. Then he turned back to the keyboard and ran his thumb, nail down, along the keys from left to right, the whole keyboard.

Eileen thought of Mr. Poole, of the mellow tone of his voice when he talked of the ivory keys on the old auditorium piano.

"Tell me what you really thought of the piece I just played, Eileen."

Even if you bought it, you have no right to keep it all to yourself, Eileen thought. You should have left the piano at home with me, because I need it too. You shouldn't have been so selfish and mean. She looked at Daddy and shrugged.

"Want me to play it again?" Daddy turned to the keyboard, and without waiting for an answer, he played.

Eileen thought of putting her fingers in her ears so she couldn't hear. But she wasn't a little kid; she couldn't do things like that. She looked away, at the wall. The music started like a low rumble, distant and worried. A threat without any teeth. And it grew and began to move, up and down the keyboard, the right hand getting playful. But the left hand lagged behind, a sad memory tugging at the center of the song. And slowly the hands listened to each other and cooperated and wove the music into a net that caught Eileen off guard. She didn't want to like this music. But she couldn't help it. It seemed familiar, like everything Daddy had ever played for her but at the same time distinct. It was rough and uneven, but undeniably beautiful. The music ended. Eileen breathed hard. She stepped across to the piano bench.

Daddy turned to her. He folded his hands in his lap. "Well?" he asked softly.

"Yes," said Eileen.

"Yes, you liked it?"

"Yes."

A smile spread across Daddy's face. "I'm glad."

Eileen couldn't help but smile back. "Why should you care if I like it?"

"I wrote it."

Eileen looked at her father, astounded. "You wrote such a wonderful thing?"

"I've been composing for years." Daddy reached out his hand and pulled Eileen to sit on the bench beside him. "But I never got anywhere just snatching a few hours late at night when you and your mother were in bed. When I finally had the piano moved here, it was like a revelation. I can test out a melody anytime I please. Anytime I have an inspiration. And I got this together. It's not finished yet. I know it's still ragged in places. But it's getting there."

"It's more than getting there."

"Oh, say it again." Daddy grinned. "Praise me to the skies."

"It's a masterpiece."

Daddy laughed.

"You'll be famous."

Daddy howled with pleasure.

"Daddy . . ." Eileen waited while Daddy calmed down. When he was looking steadily at her, she spoke. "I was mad when you took the piano . . ."

Daddy's face went solemn. "I can't afford to buy another one right now. But I'll save the money and I'll get you one as soon as I can. You're big, Eileen. You understand."

Eileen wanted to agree. She wanted to say that it was okay, that yes, now she understood why Daddy had needed the piano so bad. She wanted to act grown up. But she didn't feel grown up. And Daddy hadn't acted grown up, had he? "You should have told me you were taking it."

Daddy spread his fingers tensely on his knees. "I did. I told you I was taking my things."

"Your things." Eileen tried to stay still as a tree, to not show any emotion, nothing at all. But her head was shaking no. It was shaking harder and harder. "You know how much I love this piano. You know. You used to listen to me play. You used to tell me how good I was. You know!"

"Like I said, this piano is my buddy."

Eileen clenched her jaw. "It's mine too."

She crossed her arms on her chest and hugged herself tight. "You stole it."

"Eileen." Daddy's voice was harsh.

"You stole it!" Eileen was half shocked by her own words. But now she knew they were true. Daddy might hate her if she said them—he might never let her come spend the weekend with him again—but she had to say them. She spoke louder. "You stole it and you know it." She trembled with rage.

Daddy dropped his face in his left hand and breathed slowly and loudly. Eileen could see his Adam's apple move as he swallowed. He looked up at last. "I should have talked more with you about it. But I had to take it."

He reached for her hand. Eileen clasped her own arms tighter. He shook his head ruefully. "I'm sorry I didn't explain it to you."

It was more than that he didn't explain it. He had devastated her. And it hurt so much. She looked slowly around the room. This was Daddy's life now. She wanted to hate it. But as her eyes moved across the couch to the books on the boards, her anger subsided. The small apartment now seemed pathetic and half empty, except for the piano. And Daddy seemed somehow half empty too. He looked almost as hurt as she felt. Eileen moved close till she pressed against Daddy's side. "What I don't understand is why you couldn't compose after dinner all along. You could have come home and done whatever you wanted."

"It wouldn't have worked."

"Yes, it would. You came home and played Beethoven. You could have come home and played your own pieces. No one would have stopped you. You could move back now. I'll explain to Mom and we won't bother you. She'll love it just as much as—"

"Stop, Eileen."

"But—"

"Stop it. You can't keep doing this. I cannot just come back. What happens between your mother and me is between us. You can't change it. It's not your business."

"Whose business is it, if it isn't mine?" Eileen stood up, shaking again.

"Things change, Eileen."

"They don't have to. You changed them."

"People can't control every damn thing that happens to them."

"Our family isn't every damn thing. It's . . . it's everything. And you changed everything."

"No. It isn't everything, Eileen."

"To me it is." Eileen fought to keep her voice from rising into a scream. "You left me. We were happy together, the three of us. And you left me. Me."

"I didn't leave you—"

"You live here now. And I don't."

Daddy took Eileen's hand. She pulled away. He stood up and drew her into his arms, close against his chest. "We are all separate. We come together when we can, when we get pleasure out of it and when we can bear it. But we don't owe each other our lives. I love you, Eileen. But I don't owe you the family. You can't keep trying to make me feel guilty. I love you, even if I can't do everything you want. If you don't understand that, that's too bad. But you have to accept it."

"I won't accept it." She pulled herself free from Daddy's arms. "Why do I always have to accept everything?" She stomped her foot.

Daddy walked to the couch. Eileen's leopard costume lay inside out, half on the couch, half on the floor, where she had thrown it when she took it off after trick-or-treating. "You're tired, Eileen. Want to sleep in the leopard costume?"

"Did Mom tell you that?"

"Did Mom tell me what?"

"That I could sleep in the costume."

"No. I just thought it might be a nice idea. It's soft and cozy and you can pretend you're in the jungle."

"She had the same idea. You see? You won't admit it, but you think alike."

Daddy laughed sadly. "Go take a bath. Then put on the costume and I'll tuck you in bed."

Eileen snatched the leopard costume from Daddy's hands and walked swiftly past to the bathroom. She ran a hot tub and climbed in. Daddy had said you can't control every damn thing that happens to you. That's exactly what Eileen had been thinking yesterday—how Mr. Poole couldn't control the fact that he'd been poor as a kid. And Mrs. Tilly's daughter Kit couldn't control the fact that she couldn't get pregnant. And Eileen couldn't control the fact that Mom and Daddy were getting divorced.

But it was all so unfair. So unfair and rotten. Eileen clenched her teeth against the burn in her eyes. Rotten, rotten, rotten.

She lathered her feet and legs, rubbing hard and fast at first, and then, gradually, slow and soft. She put the soap bar back in its little dish and lay back, unmoving, letting all the fight dissolve out of her, until the water was barely warm and the skin on her fingers puckered. This was life. It was changing around her, and there were only small parts of it that she could control.

The recurring melody in the piece Daddy had composed ran through her head. It was beautiful, truly beautiful. Daddy was a composer. In this strange apartment, in this new life, he was someone he'd yearned to be for years.

Who was Eileen in this new life?

She rinsed off and wrapped herself in the big towel. She pulled on the leopard costume. Mom and Daddy were right: it felt cuddly against her clean, bare skin. It gave a sense of safety. And she was sleepy.

She came back into the living room.

Daddy had opened the sofa bed and turned down the covers for her. "Climb in."

Eileen crawled under the covers and lay back. "Daddy, do you think Chopin's preludes have endings?"

Daddy sat on the edge of the sofa bed. "That's a good question. I guess I know what you mean. He'll start a melody and hint at one direction, then he won't go that way. When he finishes, it isn't really over. You're right."

"I'm not the one who noticed it. Someone else did. He said Chopin leaves him wondering."

" 'Him,' huh? Your friend's a boy."

"Sort of."

"Sort of?" Daddy lifted both eyebrows. "How can someone be sort of a boy?"

"Don't ask."

"Well, your friend has a good sense of music."

That was true; Eileen knew that Mr. Poole understood music, whether he could read the notes on a page or not. "Mozart's not like that at all, is he, Daddy? Mozart always finishes things."

"I agree. Probably that's because he composed a lot of

operas. He tried to tell stories about characters. So even when he composed a piano piece, he would evoke a consistent mood. He's more calculated and organized than Chopin."

Daddy's words made complete sense to Eileen. "I like that," she said with decision. "I like that about Mozart a lot."

"I know you do. It appeals to your rational mind."

"I want to learn a new Mozart piece to play for my friend." Eileen pictured Mr. Poole sweeping, then stopping his work to listen closer. The thought made her happy. "Will you help me choose?"

"Sure. I have something I bet you'll love."

Eileen smiled. "Then I bet he'll love it too."

ten

CANARY SEEDS

*H*ere, chew on these." Stephanie opened her fist slowly. A small pile of seeds formed on Eileen's palm.

Eileen looked at the seeds. "What are these?"

Stephanie brushed off her hands and pulled on her gloves. "Birdseed. Canary, to be exact." She smoothed her sweater lovingly. "My favorite sweater has a new hole." She peered closely at a dime-size hole near her wrist. "I don't know how much longer it's going to last."

"I'm sorry," said Eileen. "I have an old pair of shorts I love too." She sighed and looked at the pile of seeds again. "Why are you giving me canary food?"

"To help you be musical."

"What?" I'm already musical, thought Eileen.

"You're going to the auditorium to play piano, right? On that big old ugly piano, you'll need to be extra musical. I have to run home."

Eileen felt a sudden urge to defend the piano. It had a good, rich tone after all. It was resonant. But, really, what did it matter what Stephanie thought of it? All that mattered was what Eileen thought. She sniffed the seeds. "How will canary seeds help me be musical?"

Stephanie struggled into the overcoat she had brought today.

"Well, canaries sing better than any other birds, according to my dad."

Eileen shook her head. It was hard not to laugh at some of the nutty things Stephanie said.

"Chew on them and see what happens. I have to get home as fast as I can and gobble up Milk Duds."

"Milk Duds?" said Eileen weakly.

"That's all that's left of the Halloween candy. My mom said she's going to throw out all the rest of the candy after dinner tonight. So I've been eating like a pig so there won't be anything for her to throw out."

"I thought you didn't like Milk Duds," said Eileen.

"I don't. But it's the principle of the thing."

Eileen laughed. "You're goofy."

"No, I'm not. My mom has to be kept in line or she'll tell me what to do when I start dating, and all my sister's work of breaking her in will be lost."

"Dating? Who'd go out with you?"

"Lots of guys," said Stephanie.

"Who?" asked Eileen.

"Milo, for one."

"Milo!" squawked Eileen. "He was picking fluff balls off his sweater all day again today. If you went out with him, your yellow sweater would be picked to pieces in a week."

"Okay, not Milo. But we both know he's nice. I heard you tell him his weapon project was good the other day. Anyway, I didn't say I was going to start dating today. But it'll happen eventually. To you too."

Eileen sniffed at the seeds again. She put a pinch in her mouth and crushed them between her teeth. "Yuck."

"Just wait and see," said Stephanie.

"I've got to go now."

"Bye." Stephanie walked backward, waving.

Eileen watched Stephanie go and marveled that she didn't trip over her loose laces. Her thoughts turned to Mr. Poole. She hadn't seen him since last Friday, and she sort of missed him. She put another pinch of birdseed in her mouth and chewed busily. It stuck in the grooves of her teeth. She poured her handful of birdseed into her pocket.

Eileen came down the dark aisle of the auditorium swiftly and went to move the piano bench in. But it was already in. Had Mr. Poole arranged it for her? Most likely no one else had used the piano since last Friday. Eileen sat down and closed her eyes. The piano keys felt thick. Was that just because she knew they were ivory? She played her scales. Her fingers flew over the keys. She was accustomed now to the loose action of the piano. And today it was exhilarating.

The lights went on. Eileen opened her eyes to watch Mr. Poole cross the front of the auditorium and get his broom, which was leaning against the wall. "Hi, Mr. Poole."

He smiled. "Hello, Eileen."

The little seeds between her teeth bothered her. She moved her mouth sideways like a cow chewing cud.

"Is that gum in your mouth? One of my most unfavorite jobs is scraping gum off the bottom of desks."

"It's canary seeds." Eileen reached into her pocket and extended a palm of seeds toward Mr. Poole. "See?"

Mr. Poole came down the stage steps and walked over to Eileen's hand, carrying the broom. A smile spread slowly across his face. "You practicing to become a bird?"

Eileen laughed. "It's my friend's idea."

"You got an odd friend."

"It's an experiment. They're supposed to make me more musical. You can have some if you want."

Mr. Poole examined the seeds. "No thanks."

Eileen put the seeds away again. "I'm going to play now."

Mr. Poole nodded. "And I'm going to sweep."

Eileen sat up straight and opened the Brimhall music book to "Cast Your Fate to the Wind." Mr. Gilbert had said that playing popular songs would be a nice balance to the rags of Scott Joplin and the classics of Mozart. Eileen thought this song was pretty. She played carefully and steadily once through to get the notes straight. Then she went through a second time, trying to pay attention to intonation. That's what Mr. Gilbert had told her to focus on—getting the diminuendos and crescendos right. Playing fortissimo and then pianissimo. It was easy to think about intonation when the notes were so simple.

As Eileen turned to Joplin, she smiled to herself. "Maple Leaf Rag" was becoming a friend. A new friend yet, because she had to do each hand separately twice through before she could put both hands together, but still a friend. She played and counted. Then she played and let the beat come on its own, trusting her hands to feel their way.

Eileen shut that music book and put the sheet music Daddy had lent her on the piano: Mozart's Sonata in F Major. Daddy was right—Eileen loved it. He'd played it for her over and over at his house last weekend. Mr. Poole was now sweeping through the rows of seats. Eileen called out, "I'm going to try a new sonata. It might not sound great."

"Go ahead and play," said Mr. Poole. He took his broom and walked down the side aisle to the far corner of the auditorium. "I can hear you from here. I'll sweep and you'll play."

"I'll make a lot of mistakes."

"Then you'll fix them," said Mr. Poole. He swept. "Go on now."

Eileen played.

The sonata turned out not to be all that hard, really, but it was a challenge anyway. Some of the little melodies on the right hand seemed to blare out on their own, as though the rest of the music was just hanging around waiting for them. If she got those melodies right, fast enough and clear enough and loud enough, the whole piece came alive, vivid and exciting.

When she finished her second time through, Mr. Poole clapped.

Eileen swiveled to look at him. She smiled. "I thought you'd like this. It'll get a lot better once I learn it."

"It makes me think of horns. Like in those hunting scenes in movies, where people on horses blow the little horns."

Eileen laughed. "You're right." She turned back to the piano and played the sonata one more time. Then she arranged all her music in a stack beside her on the bench. She had finished practicing everything she had wanted to.

She looked around. Mr. Poole had gone back to sweeping. He had his back to her, as though practice was over. But Eileen was all wound up from the thrill of the sonata. And it was still early—Mrs. Tilly wouldn't expect her yet. So she could keep playing.

She rested both hands lightly on the piano keys. Then she fingered out a melody on the right hand. It wasn't too good. So she changed it. And changed again. And found something she liked. She played around with chords on the left hand. She got one that was okay. She put both hands together.

"That's coming along," said Mr. Poole. He came and stood beside her. "Hmm."

"Hmm what?"

"I don't know. It's nice."

But it could be better. Eileen knew that. She fiddled around with both hands. It wasn't getting anywhere. She tried again, using only her middle finger and thumb on the left hand this time. That made all the difference. Wow.

Eileen started over. It was fun. She was actually making up a melody, and it was so much fun. "Do you like it?"

"Do I like it?" Mr. Poole rubbed at the big bumpy knuckles of his left hand and looked up as if in thought. "Do I like it?" He smiled down at Eileen. "I like this tune. It's just right."

Eileen giggled. She counted as she played it again. "There's only eight notes in the whole thing. I guess it's kind of short."

"That's okay. So are you. A short composer."

Eileen laughed. "My father's a composer."

"You didn't tell me that the other day."

"I didn't know it."

"You didn't know your own father's a composer? Well, is he famous?"

"Not yet." Eileen hesitated. The piece Daddy had composed was wonderful. But a part of her didn't want to admit it. She was still angry at him. "But he's good," she conceded.

"Yup, those genes again."

Eileen blushed happily. "I'm not a composer. I'm just fooling around. It's fun."

"Good. I'm looking forward to listening to it grow." Mr. Poole wagged his finger. "That is, just as long as you don't fly away."

"What?" said Eileen, mystified.

"Eatin' all them canary seeds."

eleven

A BUSINESS DEAL

*E*ileen hummed her own special tune as she bounded up the walk to Mrs. Tilly's house. She couldn't wait to take Jared into her arms and sing it for him. She imagined Jared's fat little face all creased in a smile. Eileen rang the bell and danced from foot to foot.

Mrs. Tilly opened the door. Her arm was in a sling. "Hello, Eileen dear." She stepped back so Eileen could pass.

"Oh, Mrs. Tilly, what happened?" Now Eileen could see the cast that went from under Mrs. Tilly's elbow down to her hand and around her thumb. Her fingers stuck out at the bottom. "Oh, no."

Mrs. Tilly smiled bravely. "I am a poor duck, aren't I? At least it's my left wrist and not my right." She closed the door behind Eileen and leaned on it for a moment. Then she stood up straight and marched into the living room. "I haven't been able to do much of anything today." She paused and wrinkled her nose at her cast, then she shook her head, as if to get rid of something distasteful. "But I can still chat, at least."

Eileen looked around. "Where's Jared?"

"Little Jared had to go to a baby-sitter."

Eileen was shocked. "Why?"

"Well, this arm, of course." Mrs. Tilly sank into the couch. "I'm not supposed to lift anything heavier than my purse for a week. And after that I have to be careful."

Eileen looked at the cast in dismay. "Do you have to keep it in a sling all the time?"

"No. It's not supposed to be in a sling at all." Mrs. Tilly made tsking noises under her breath. "They told me to use the arm as much as I can or my elbow will get stiff. But it hurts so much less in the sling that I guess I've been naughty."

"I think you should take off the sling," said Eileen.

Mrs. Tilly gave Eileen an even look. "You're probably

right." She took off the sling and exercised her arm slowly up and down.

"Does it hurt terribly?"

"Not so bad. I complain just because it's such a disappointment and annoyance. You have no idea how hard it was to make baby-sitting arrangements on such short notice. I can't wait till it's healed."

"Milo, this boy in my class, had a broken arm, and he wore his cast for only three weeks."

"Three weeks?" said Mrs. Tilly. "Is that all?"

"Or maybe six, I'm not sure. But it wasn't long at all."

"Well, at my age bones heal slowly. I'll have this on a lot longer than six weeks, I'm afraid. And then there will be the next time."

"What do you mean?"

"It's a long story." Mrs. Tilly sighed and looked past Eileen. "That spider plant needs watering."

Eileen went to the kitchen and got a glass of water. She came back and watered the plant. "How did you break your arm?"

"I was clipping back the chrysanthemums and I just slipped on some wet leaves and that was it."

"You fell?"

"Yes."

"What bad luck," said Eileen. "I fall a lot, but I never break anything."

"Your bones are flexible. Mine are thin and brittle. I've got . . ." Mrs. Tilly hesitated. "I've got osteoporosis." The way she whispered, it made it sound like the most terrible thing in the world.

"Osteoporosis," said Eileen slowly. "What is it?"

"A disease. My bones keep getting thinner and thinner. On the X ray I could hardly see them at all. To think I didn't even know it, and I've been racing around doing anything I pleased as though I were as fit as a fiddle. The doctor says I'm awfully young for this disease." Mrs. Tilly made a little grimace. "At least I'm young for something."

"Your arm will get better and you'll get the cast off and you'll race around again."

"If I do, I'll get another broken bone. They said it's going to be chronic now. I'll break one bone after another."

Eileen opened her mouth in horror.

Mrs. Tilly looked at her and straightened her glasses. "There now, I've scared you. It's not that bad. A lot of women get it. If I'm careful, I'll get along fine."

"How did you get it?"

"I never drank milk when I was a kid. I didn't like it."

"And because you didn't drink milk then, your bones break now?" asked Eileen.

"It's the calcium. They say you need it when you're young."

"It's not fair." Eileen shook her head vehemently. She walked back and forth in front of the couch. "It's not fair that you should be sick now for something you didn't do when you were a kid."

"Don't get so worked up." Mrs. Tilly patted the cushion beside her. "Here, come sit down."

Eileen sat beside Mrs. Tilly. "There's nothing you can do about it?"

"Well, I'll be a lot more careful from now on, you can bet on that." Mrs. Tilly wiggled the fingers that stuck out of her cast.

"You said you haven't been able to do much today. Is there something I can help you with now?"

"That's an idea. Do you cook?"

"Sure. I mean, I'm not good at it or anything, but I can follow directions."

"That's good enough. I was supposed to go to a book club tonight, and I wanted to bring a spicy jalapeño-artichoke dip. I was just trying to make it when you came. But everything is so hard with this cast on."

"What are jalapeños?"

"Spicy peppers." Mrs. Tilly laughed at the expression on Eileen's face. "There's cheese in it too, so that keeps it from being too spicy. It's good. Really."

Eileen followed Mrs. Tilly into the kitchen. She looked at the lineup of ingredients on the counter: a plate with two skinny green peppers that had been grilled, a small jar of pickled artichoke hearts, a package of cream cheese, a can of grated Parmesan cheese. Mrs. Tilly took the top off her food processor. She looked at Eileen expectantly. Eileen dumped in the peppers, artichoke hearts, and cream cheese, one after the other. "How much grated cheese?"

"A good healthy sprinkling, please. And salt and pepper."

Eileen obeyed happily. There was something soothing about cooking with Mrs. Tilly. She put the top on the food processor, and Mrs. Tilly turned the dial.

After a few seconds, Mrs. Tilly turned it off. She pointed to an iron frying pan on the stove top. "Would you scrape it all into the pan, please?"

Eileen carefully scraped out the mix with a rubber spatula. Mrs. Tilly turned on the oven and opened it. Eileen put the frying pan on a rack in the center of the oven. Mrs. Tilly closed the oven door and hummed something Eileen knew. Eileen joined in. "What's that called?"

" 'The Bridge on the River Kwai.' " Mrs. Tilly cocked her head. "I'm surprised you know it."

"Stephanie's big sister plays it on the flute. Want to hear another tune?" Eileen hummed her own tune.

"That's nice. I don't know it. But I like it." Mrs. Tilly opened the refrigerator. "See that bag on the top shelf? Can you reach it? You're such a wonderful help."

Eileen set the bag on the counter and opened it. A bunch of vegetables sat there.

"They need to be washed," said Mrs. Tilly.

Eileen rinsed the snap peas and scrubbed the baby carrots and radishes. She put them on the counter.

"That should do it." Mrs. Tilly smiled. "It'll only be another few minutes. Why don't you hum me that tune again?"

Eileen hummed.

Mrs. Tilly nodded. "Yes, I like it. Now take those pot holders there and be careful." She opened the oven door.

"Is the dip done already?"

"All it needs to do is get hot enough to make the tastes blend. Everything in it is cooked already."

Eileen took out the pan carefully while Mrs. Tilly put a trivet on the kitchen table. Eileen set the pan on the trivet.

"Shall we sneak a little taste just to see if it's good enough to serve to others?" Mrs. Tilly picked up a peapod and dipped it in the mix. She ate it. "Mmm."

Eileen mimicked Mrs. Tilly with a baby carrot. "Good," she mumbled with her mouth full. And it was. Her tongue tingled, but in a nice way. "You make good food."

"Thank you." Mrs. Tilly laughed. "But you made it this time. Cooking is a pleasure. I watched an interesting video at Kit's house on Saturday night when I was baby-sitting. It's called *Tampopo*. It means *dandelion*. It's about a woman who decides to make the perfect bowl of Japanese noodle soup. I enjoyed it so much that Kit said she's going to get me another movie about cooking for the next time I baby-sit called *Babette's Feast*."

Eileen thought about Mrs. Tilly baby-sitting, watching a VCR. "Do you miss Jared?"

"Well, I just saw him Saturday and it's only Monday." Mrs. Tilly ran her tongue across her teeth under her top lip. "But I suppose I do miss him a bit already. It was fun having him here in the afternoons. And it's certainly complicated for poor Kit now. Jared has to be carted off to a baby-sitter's house. But the baby-sitter won't keep Jared long enough, so a neighbor has to pick him up. To tell the truth, it's awful now."

Eileen thought about that. Then she looked Mrs. Tilly square in the face. "What time does Jared come in the afternoon? I mean, what time did he used to come?"

"Kit dropped him off around three. Just a few minutes before you'd come. She starts her nursing shift at the clinic at four. Four to midnight, that's her shift. She works very hard. Jim always picked Jared up at six-fifteen or so, on his way home from work."

"Then it should all work out," said Eileen with determination.

"What should all work out?"

"Mom doesn't come home from work till almost six anyway, so she wouldn't mind if I stayed till Jim got here. And I can walk a little faster on my way home, so that I get here by the time Kit drops him off." Eileen leaned toward Mrs. Tilly. "Jared can keep coming, and I can help you take care of him."

Mrs. Tilly looked at Eileen, then down at the dip between them, then at Eileen again. "What if you have something else to do?"

Besides practicing in the auditorium, nothing else really mattered. "I never have anything else to do."

"What about Tuesdays?" said Mrs. Tilly. "You never come on Tuesdays."

"That's because I have an hour piano lesson and Stephanie goes first. But I can arrange with Stephanie so I go first. Then I can run here from Mr. Gilbert's house. He lives right around the corner."

"Yes, I know Mr. Gilbert." Mrs. Tilly tapped her fingernail against her bottom teeth anxiously. "Do you really mean it? Would you come every day, Monday through Friday? Would you be reliable?"

"Yes."

"And you can do all the things that need to be done," said Mrs. Tilly, with rising excitement. "You can change him and put him down for a nap. And keep him happy. Yes, you can do it, Eileen." She moved her right hand up and down along her cast. "All right. What's your rate?"

"Rate?"

"I'll pay you. This is a business deal."

"But I don't want money," said Eileen. "I love to play with Jared."

"There must be something you'd like to save up money

for," said Mrs. Tilly. "Think about it. A person should be paid for honest work. And child care is honest work."

Eileen's heart beat fast. "I want to buy a piano."

Mrs. Tilly's face fell. "Well, that will take some saving up. That's quite a large purchase."

"How about a dollar an hour?" said Eileen. "That's what my mother pays me for raking leaves."

Mrs. Tilly patted Eileen's hand, then sat up straight again. "Pretty paltry pay. How about twenty dollars a week?"

Eileen nodded. "You've got a deal."

twelve

FIGHTING

*E*ileen jiggled her fork against the edge of her plate. She had set the table a half hour ago and Mom wasn't home yet. Maybe she should call Daddy. But Daddy would still be at the office and it would only worry him. And then Mom would get mad at Eileen for making a big deal out of nothing and maybe she'd even think that Eileen was trying to get Daddy to worry about Mom. Maybe Eileen should just call Mom's office. Only she'd never called there yet, and she was shy to. What if someone nasty answered the phone? At least at Daddy's office she knew everyone. And Mom was new on the job;

maybe Eileen would get Mom in trouble if she called. Eileen looked at the clock. 6:42. All right, she'd call. She flipped through the Rolodex. She dialed. The phone rang and rang and rang.

"Eileen, Eileen," called Mom, slamming the front door shut behind her.

Eileen sat back down at the table and waited.

Mom came into the kitchen and plopped a white bag on the table. "Here," she said, pulling off her gloves and hat breathlessly. "I picked up subs on the way home. You've already set the table. That's so sweet of you." Mom went back into the hall to hang her coat. "It was such a busy afternoon," she called from the hall. "Mr. Harnatt got a big order at the last minute and I had to stay to fill out all the invoices." She bustled back into the kitchen. "Well, how are you, honey?"

Eileen jiggled her fork against her plate and didn't look at her mother.

Mom opened the bag and put a cellophane-wrapped sandwich on Eileen's plate and another on her own. She took two glasses out of the cupboard and filled them with ice. Then she pulled a bottle of Coke out of the white bag. "Is something the matter?"

"I'll have milk," said Eileen, not looking up.

"Milk? I bought Coke as a treat. We never have soda, Eileen. Don't you want some?"

"You want all my bones to break when I'm sixty?"

"What are you talking about?" Mom sank into her chair and leaned back. "I'm so tired."

Eileen finally looked at her. "If I don't eat cheese and drink milk now, I'll break all my bones when I'm old. Like Mrs. Tilly."

"Mrs. Tilly?"

"She broke her wrist," said Eileen. "She has a disease."

"Osteoporosis."

"That's it."

"Poor Sarah. I'll have to go see if I can help her."

"Help her? You can't even make dinner for us."

"My goodness, you're certainly shooting from the hip tonight." Mom rubbed at her nose. "There's no need to be so hard on me. I had to work late, Eileen."

"I know." Eileen jiggled her fork against her plate again. "I'm the one who sat here wondering if you'd died in a car accident."

Mom reached out her hand and took the fork from Eileen's fist. She tried to take Eileen's hand in hers.

Eileen dropped her hand into her lap and looked away. "I'm sorry. I should have called," said Mom.

Eileen nodded.

"I'll call next time."

Eileen looked at her mother and shook her head in disgust. She unwrapped the sandwich. At least it was Italian cold cuts. Mom poured Coke in both glasses.

"I said I wanted milk."

Mom sighed. "I didn't have a chance to go shopping. We don't have any milk."

"And what am I supposed to do for breakfast? Eat my cereal dry?"

"I'll go out after dinner. You can come with me if you like. It can be a little adventure."

"Mom." Eileen took a sip of Coke. The fizz went up her nose. She coughed. "I'm too old to think a trip to the grocery store is an adventure."

"Even if we stop at Nifty Fifties afterward for a malt?"

Eileen almost smiled, then she caught herself. "Okay. I'll come."

"Why such a grouch? Did something happen today?"

"No." Eileen took a big bite of sandwich. It was dry. She washed it down with Coke.

"So Mrs. Tilly broke her wrist. I guess she won't be able to take care of her grandson now."

"I'm going to help her," said Eileen. "She's paying me twenty dollars a week."

"Twenty dollars. You'll be rich. What will you do with it all?"

"I'm going to help Daddy buy me a new piano."

"A new piano costs a couple of thousand dollars, Eileen. No one's going to get you a new piano."

Eileen took a gulp of Coke. "I don't want a brand-new one." She listened to her words and suddenly realized they were true. "I want an old one with real ivory keys."

Mom smiled. "I love old ivory keys, too. Okay, we'll keep a lookout in the classifieds. There are always old pianos for sale. Sometimes they're cheap too."

"How cheap?"

"Even a couple of hundred dollars. We'll keep looking till we find the right one. How much did your father say he'd pitch in?"

"He didn't. He just said he'd buy me a piano when he could. But you could talk to him and get him to say how much. Maybe he could help us look in the paper . . ."

"You can talk to him, Eileen. Not me."

Eileen pushed her plate away. "This sub stinks."

"They're not very good, are they?" Mom looked around. "I think there's some peanut butter left." She stood up and went to the cupboard. She held out a jar. "Want a peanut butter and jelly sandwich?"

"I'm not hungry."

"Eileen, you're a growing girl. Just because I didn't do the shopping and you can't eat what you want doesn't mean I'm going to allow you to skip a meal entirely. Do you want peanut butter?"

"I ate jalapeño-artichoke dip with vegetables at Mrs. Tilly's."

"Oh. Well, in that case, I think I'll just make do with my sub." Mom put the jar away and sat down again.

"You won't even try to talk to him, will you?"

Mom drank some Coke. "Eileen, I don't want to hear any more about this."

"You're going to tell me to accept it, aren't you?"

"I don't have to. You just told yourself," said Mom.

"Let's go shopping," said Eileen.

Mom put the dishes on the counter. She filled the sink with sudsy water.

"Let the dishes wait," said Eileen.

"It hardly takes any time at all to clean them." Mom lowered the two glasses carefully into the water.

"I hate the way you clean up all the time. You're compulsive about it. The minute I take off my clothes, you whisk them off to the washer. The minute I finish my last spoonful of Chex, you drop the bowl in the sink. The minute—"

"Enough. I get the picture." Mom rinsed the glasses and put the two dishes into the sudsy water. "What's gotten into you? You never make speeches. But ever since I walked in that door, you've been lecturing me."

"All that cleaning and everything. You drive me crazy."

"Eileen, I've always kept a clean house. I'm not about to fall apart now. Maybe, just maybe, you're annoyed for other reasons. Did something go wrong at school today?"

"Nothing went wrong. It's you."

Mom rinsed the glasses and set them in the dish rack. "So family is getting you down."

"Not family. You. You, you, you." Eileen knew her words were cruel; she hated them. But she couldn't stop talking. "You drive me crazy. Daddy doesn't."

Mom turned around and dried her hands on the dish towel. Her cheeks were flushed with anger. "How can he? You don't live with him. You only see him every other weekend. Face it."

Eileen felt like she'd been slapped. She stood up.

Mom walked past her into the hall. "You can finish the dishes later. Let's go shopping."

Eileen didn't move. She was afraid if she did, she'd shatter into a thousand pieces. She couldn't tell if she wanted to yell or cry, but she thought if she started either, she'd never stop. No, she wouldn't cry with Mom. And she wouldn't cry with Daddy.

"Hurry up," Mom called. Then she added in a softer tone, "Oh, I saw Stephanie's mother today at lunchtime."

"Mmm," mumbled Eileen. Slowly she followed Mom into the hall.

"We arranged for Stephanie to spend the night here Friday."

"You didn't!" shouted Eileen. "You couldn't have. I told you not to."

"Eileen, what's the matter?" Mom stared at Eileen with bewilderment on her face. "Stephanie's your best friend. She hasn't spent the night since school started."

"How could I invite her here when I never knew if you and Daddy would have one of your freeze-outs? You at one end of the table and him at the other, not speaking to each other. You did that all through September."

"Well, we can't have a freeze-out now. Daddy won't be here."

"I know," said Eileen. "That's just it. Daddy won't be here. And Stephanie will know." Eileen leaned against the wall. Her body felt so heavy, she could hardly stand. "Stephanie will know."

Mom's face went pale. "Oh, Eileen, I didn't realize you hadn't told . . . I'm so sorry. I'll call her mother. I'll say this weekend won't work. And later, when you're ready for Stephanie to . . ." Mom stopped.

Eileen saw tears fill her mother's eyes. She moved toward her instinctively. "No. I'll take care of it, Mom," she whispered. "Thanks, anyway." She stood straight in the warm circle of her mother's arms. Slowly, slowly she bent her neck and let her cheek rest against Mom's shoulder.

thirteen

SECRETS

urry up, Eileen. You're the slowest eater I know. Everyone else has gone out to recess and we won't have any recess left at all, at the rate you're eating." Stephanie rolled her pear around her lunch tray.

"Go on without me," said Eileen. It was Friday. All week long Eileen had concentrated on practicing the piano and rushing back to take care of Jared and then doing her schoolwork. She had concentrated on everything but Stephanie. And now it was Friday, and tonight Stephanie was coming over to Eileen's house to spend the night and Daddy wouldn't be there and Stephanie would know. "Go on."

Stephanie stopped rolling her pear. "Aw, it's okay. I shouldn't rush you. Eating slow helps the digestion and it keeps you calm. You eat less that way."

"And have thinner thighs," said Eileen.

"Yes."

"Mind if I get under your feet there, young ladies?" Mr. Poole stood across the lunch table from them. He smiled.

"Hi, Mr. Poole." Eileen lifted her feet distractedly.

Mr. Poole pursed his lips. "On second thought, you can put your feet back down. Looks like that sandwich is going mighty slow. Maybe I'll just go vacuum the library and let you girls finish in peace. I can sweep here later."

"Thanks, Mr. Poole."

Stephanie wriggled around on the lunch bench. "I'm bringing my new sleeping bag tonight. It's dusty rose, the color, I mean. It cost twenty-two dollars. And I earned every penny of it."

Eileen thought of her job taking care of Jared and the twenty dollars a week she was earning. She wouldn't tell Stephanie about that right now—she wouldn't make her jealous. "Sounds great."

"It is." Stephanie tapped on her pear. "And I helped pay for my new shoes. You haven't said a word about them."

Eileen inspected the shoes with admiration. They were black patent leather. "They're fancy."

"My mother got sick of me refusing to tie my laces. She said it was time I started to act a little older, more graceful and whatever. Anyway, in middle school a lot of girls wear this kind of shoe. And they're pretty, don't you think?"

"Totally."

"So what are we going to do tonight?"

"My mother bought another blueberry muffin mix," said Eileen.

"Hmm, good." Stephanie picked up the pear and rubbed it on her shirt. "Do you really like blueberries?"

Eileen looked at Stephanie, surprised. "Why?"

"Well, do you?"

"Actually, no," said Eileen. "But I love the color of the muffins, and it's so funny the way they make your teeth blue."

"I don't like them either," said Stephanie. "I sprinkle sugar on top, so that I can't taste them."

The girls giggled.

"When we're old, we'll sprinkle sugar on top of tomatoes," said Stephanie.

Eileen shook her head in disbelief. "What?"

"That's what old people do. Their taste buds die one by one. But the taste for sweets is the last to go. Old people sprinkle sugar on top of everything so that at least their food tastes like something."

Eileen thought of Mrs. Tilly losing her taste buds and not being able to enjoy her spicy jalapeño-artichoke dip. How terrible. It had to be wrong. "Someone crazy told you that."

"My old baby-sitter. She did volunteer work at the West End Nursing Home, so she knew all sorts of weird things that happen to you when you get old."

"Did she know about osteoporosis?"

"What's that?" said Stephanie.

"It's when your bones rot away."

"How awful."

"I've been thinking of reading up on it," said Eileen on an impulse.

"I'll go with you to the public library," said Stephanie.

"Stephanie," said Eileen in a slow, small voice.

"Have you met her, the new librarian? She's got the coolest hair and talk about shoes! And she's got the weirdest—"

"Shut up, Stephanie."

Stephanie's eyes opened wide. She stared at Eileen.

"I need you to listen. I've got something to tell you. Something important."

"I know."

"You know?"

"Sure," said Stephanie. "If I acted real odd, wouldn't you know that I had something to tell you?"

Eileen nodded her head. "We don't have a piano anymore."

"I figured as much. What happened?"

"My father took it."

"Where?"

Eileen took a deep breath. "To his place."

"His office?"

"No, his apartment. My parents are getting a divorce."

"Oh, no," said Stephanie. "Oh, no."

Without warning, Eileen cried. She sobbed. All the tears she'd held back for the past weeks streamed down her cheeks.

Stephanie moved closer till her forehead touched Eileen's cheek. She put her arms softly around Eileen's waist.

It was a long time before Eileen could breathe normally again. "It's going to be okay," she said, scooting back just a little and brushing the tears away as they fell. "I miss him a lot. But I spend every other weekend with him. That's where I was on Halloween."

"Oh," said Stephanie. She smoothed Eileen's hair with both hands.

"I've been so unhappy. And mean."

"Mean?"

"To my mother."

"Oh," said Stephanie.

"Hateful, in fact," said Eileen, barely choking out the words. "Worse than to my father, and he's the one who left."

"Oh," said Stephanie.

"I'm sorry I kept it a secret from you. I didn't mean to. I just couldn't talk about it." Eileen looked at Stephanie. "Do you hate me for not telling you?"

"Hate you?" Stephanie wrapped her arms around Eileen again and cried. Eileen tenderly wiped Stephanie's face. "You know, I thought you hated me 'cause you never wanted me to come over anymore." Stephanie took a deep breath. "You're a much better friend than Suzanne." She dropped her hands by her sides. "I have a secret too. I'm going to get braces. After Christmas. I didn't tell you either."

"I'm sorry," said Eileen.

"So am I," said Stephanie.

"Steph," said Eileen, "you're the first person I've talked to about it who didn't tell me right away to accept it. That's all my parents can say."

Stephanie nodded. "Parents always want us to accept it when they mess things up, but they get mad when we mess up. Imagine what they'd say if we did something terrible, did some sort of science experiment in our bedrooms or something and ruined all the wallpaper, and turned to them and went, 'Hey, folks, accept it.' Ha."

"Divorce and osteoporosis," said Eileen.

Stephanie looked at Eileen doubtfully. "Divorce and osteoporosis?"

"They've both awful. But that's how it is."

Stephanie took a bite of her pear. "I know," she said, chewing, "I know what we can do tonight. We can make those blueberry muffins. Then we can carry them outside and feed them to the squirrels."

Eileen clapped. "And no one will know where the muffins went."

"And there will be all these weird squirrels running around with blue teeth," said Stephanie.

Eileen laughed. "It'll be our secret." She finished her sandwich. "Steph, will you come to the auditorium with me after school while I practice piano? I'm composing a new tune, and so far only Mr. Poole has heard the whole thing."

"Mr. Poole? You mean the custodian Mr. Poole?"

"He's got a great ear for music."

"Sure," said Stephanie.

"Oh, I hope you'll like it."

"I will," said Stephanie. "Count on it."